D0911695

PLAGUE OF GUNFIGHTERS

The coming of strangers, a sick man and a young girl, divided, the townsfolk of Gabriel. It was the revelation of just who this man was that caused the sensation. Purnell, the town marshal, was expected either to banish the strangers or bear responsibility for the trouble which must surely come. When indeed violence did explode, not only was Purnell exposed to danger, but his wife and son as well. And before long, Gabriel was torn asunder.

TOM ANSON

PLAGUE OF GUNFIGHTERS

Complete and Unabridged

LINFORD
Leicester

First published in Great Britain in 1996 by
Robert Hale Limited
London

First Linford Edition
published 1997
by arrangement with
Robert Hale Limited
London

British Library CIP Data

Anson, Tom
Plague of gunfighters.—Large print ed.—
Linford western library
1. Western stories
2. Large type books
I. Title
823.9'14 [F]

ISBN 0–7089–5130–9

Published by
F. A. Thorpe (Publishing) Ltd.
Anstey, Leicestershire

Set by Words & Graphics Ltd.
Anstey, Leicestershire
Printed and bound in Great Britain by
T. J. International Ltd., Padstow, Cornwall

This book is printed on acid-free paper

1

SHARP cries and the clumsy-booted running of men are bringing others out of doors, questioning, then pointing.

By this time the dozen horses inside Beyer's corral are circling anxiously, heads up, whickering, eyes whitening, while a rouge glow goes crawling up the sky, as though some nosey bastard might have lifted up one corner of the lid of Hell to see what was inside.

For most, this is a night which started out to be one of indifferent ordinariness but which will end by becoming *the night of the Fielding fire*, and in future will be remembered and talked about in that way.

The two-storey house on Larchmont, a street set at right-angles off Main, stands a little apart from its nearest neighbour and is aglow within, and now bang goes one upstairs window, now another, bright shards flying, men instinctively ducking away, and out come licking yellowy tongues under the sounds of their own roaring life.

In Daish's yard, in lurching lantern-light they have made good time in harnessing the stolid four that will draw the flat-deck with its iron tank and coiled canvas hose and long, seesaw pump-handle, shrouding the heads of horses that must be taken near the fire, men cursing, striking shins, shouting commands; but now they have got the heavy rig rolling.

People are inside the burning house, and one of them, a tall, strong-looking man with a dull, dented star on his black vest, his once-white shirt dirty and singed, is on the smoky stairs, yelling as he comes backing down, one forearm raised across his face, "Where the hell's Cape?"

Crouching inside the front door, a deputy, hatless, torn, blackened, answers, "Out! Cape's out!"

"Then you get gone too."

The man on the dangerous stairs has stopped retreating and will make one more flesh-searing try to get back up to the landing to get to the door up there. He will do his damnedest but he will not succeed.

Those arriving at the scene can see that the high, narrow house is fiercely alight now, one man already out, then a second, this one stumbling away from the smoking porch, while high above, hastening to the invisible sky goes a whirling host of fireflies, leaping up out of the house, roaring from the throat of the burning.

Here, approaching now, the creaking wagon and its straining team towing the dark water-tank, men yelling, cursing it onwards, no chance of fighting such a blaze and winning, intent only upon preserving other structures.

Waves of intense heat can be felt a hundred feet away.

Different people in the town will carry away different memories of this fire depending on where each happens to be at the time. Those who venture close will recall the pulsating heat and the sounds of the flames at their height and the twisting funnel of flying sparks climbing away; others further off might remember only sharp roofs and false fronts limned against the angry glow, and silhouettes of horses and men moving urgently.

High up in another house, for an awakened child, the fire is scarcely more than a mysterious glow on a window-shade, a light, brightening and fading by turns across a stained ceiling, and the sounds of distant adult voices calling, the creaking of moving wheels and the whickering of horses; and a tangy, nose-tickling smell that will hang around all the rooms in the house for days, though not quite so sharp as it is now. Other images, some of them more subtle, will stay with the child, only to emerge later in life.

Of course, even after the last vestiges of smell from the night-fire have gone from the town, there must be an enquiry, which is in fact an inquest.

★ ★ ★

The wood-pillared awning outside the red brick county courthouse and the studded double doors seem to promise an interior opulence, but that, like so many other things in this community, is an illusion.

There are long unyielding benches set row on row for the use of the general public, a couple of desks for the recorders of proceedings; and raised somewhat higher than all of these, facing the assembly, a worn, shiny desk where today sits Bolton C. Whittaker, narrow-faced, ascetic, goatee-jutting, his quick, brown-bean, intelligent eyes under prominent brows, slicing this way and that. Indubitably, he is in his own milieu, the man in charge.

Over to his left there is a place with a low brass rail in front, where the witness of the moment sits.

Little more than ten minutes after they get started, this long, dull room is smoky and darting with flies and filled with a low muttering sound and some coughing, until Bolton C. Whittaker gavels them to the nearest thing to silence that is likely to be achieved.

"Don't make me gavel again," says Whittaker, then once again points his goatee towards the man who is seated in the witness' chair, tall and big-shouldered, wearing a pale-blue shirt and a black string tie. His face, lined and sun-ravaged, bears old white scars and much newer reddish ones, healing burns, and his left arm is wrapped in gauze, the sleeve of the blue shirt having been rolled up out of the way. The dark eyes of this man are sunken but steady and unreadable, though he looks tired, hearing Whittaker continue:

"So you went in with your deputies because you believed French to be in there — Arnold John French, a wanted man?"

"Yes, that's so. We felt pretty sure he was there."

"Yes, I see. Sheriff, may we now ask how you came by that belief?"

"By various means. It came from different sources that all said the same thing." *It came from bastards who, one by one, will now be sought out.*

Beetle-browed, arrow-sharp face thrusting forward: "Utterly unreliable ones as it transpired."

The witness sits quite still, face impassive, but the hard eyes have stirred to life, listening to Whittaker's statement of the obvious.

"It would seem so."

Whittaker continues staring at the witness, perhaps even contemplating a further probing along this line, but eventually he does not, saying:

"So it turned out that once you'd got inside, there was but one occupant, a woman, Bella Fielding?"

"Yes."

"You knew this woman? I mean, you were aware of who she was?"

"I knew who she was."

"She was a long-time resident?"

"No. To my knowledge she'd been living in the town for maybe three, four months."

Whittaker sniffs, waves a languid hand in front of his face, glances around with short, sharp head-movements like some wary, grounded bird, as though he has just become conscious of the vast amount of tobacco-smoke in the room; then just as abruptly he returns his attention to the witness.

"You spoke with her? I mean, after you finally got inside the house?"

"Yes. Yes, I told her we'd come in to take Jack French."

"Come in." Whittaker repeats the words immediately as though having fully expected to hear them and now, having thus lain in wait for them, wishes to examine them further. But there is a slight pause before he says again, "*Come in* would be only the half of it, wouldn't you say? As I understand it, you had your men kick a door down and you all went on in at a run, after the woman had repeatedly refused to open it to your demands."

Now there is a certain amount of shuffling and muttering among the public benches but Whittaker, staring at the witness, appears not to notice for he does not do any gaveling.

"Yes. That was done because we — because I thought that French was in there and that Bella Fielding was set on delaying us."

Whittaker's long white fingers tease at his goatee. "But that proved not to be the case."

"It did."

The darting eyes from beneath their great brows have the glitter of glass beads.

"This man French and, er, Mrs Fielding, as I understand it, sheriff, they are — were related."

"They were cousins."

This time there arises a communal muttering and even a small laugh, all of which Whittaker cannot ignore, so he gavels accordingly and favours the entire room with a sweep of the brown-bean eyes. It is enough. The noise subsides. Even the next cough is stifled, almost apologetic. If Whittaker himself is aware of the reason for the upswell of talk when his witness said "*They were cousins*" he offers no hint of it.

The witness, however, as do his singed and blistered deputies seated in the front row, knows that *sotto voce* exchanges which doubtless are continuing in spite of Whittaker's bad mood and loud gavel, will be all of a kind. "*Real close cousins.*"

Whittaker pulls in a long breath, expels it slowly while turning papers over, putting and taking others, seeming almost disconsolate as though he might have lost some of his enthusiasm.

"And you state . . . (searching for references among the papers) you state that Bella Fielding then ran up some stairs and into a room and slammed the door and locked it."

"Yes, that's what happened." The

still-life witness with the old star pinned to his vest goes on staring back at Whittaker as though no-one else exists. The attention of everyone else is on the witness. His supporters doubtless will see him as calmly resolute, his detractors as heartless, little better than a paid gun-carrier.

"And at some point after that, a lamp got knocked over and it broke."

"Yes."

It is manifestly clear that although all of these matters have been fully recorded at an earlier time and are before Bolton C. Whittaker as he speaks, each incident is to be dissected afresh.

"Ye . . . e . . . s." Whittaker looks up. "It seems that this lamp was not knocked over by Mrs Fielding herself. Now, exactly where was it?"

"It was on a table on the landing."

"A table on the landing."

Worn carpet, peeling, match-dry wallpaper, an old cloth draped over a small table, the lighted lamp on it.

"Yes."

Whittaker's attention with all its old enthusiasm is again fixed firmly on the witness.

"So if the lamp was not knocked over by the, er, occupant, then who did knock it over?"

One of the deputies uncrosses, then recrosses his legs.

"Mr Smith."

"Deputy August Smith?"

"Yes."

"Will you please explain to us how Deputy Smith managed to do that?"

"At my orders, he went on up the stairs after her."

"After her?"

"To detain her. We still thought that Jack French might be somewhere in the house." When, unexpectedly, Whittaker makes no comment, the witness goes on, "The deputies — "

"Deputies?" Whittaker seizes the plural while it is still hot.

"Deputy Cape had also gone up the stairs."

"So, when Mrs Fielding fled upstairs, both of your deputies went rushing up after her?"

"Deputy Smith was ordered up by me. Deputy Cape followed him."

"Well now. And what exactly did you do at this point, sheriff?"

The witness takes in a restoring breath, perhaps now aware of all eyes being on him, but it is the most noticeable move he has made so far.

"I went through all the ground-floor rooms, checking them out."

"But you found no-one."

"That's correct."

"And then?"

"I came back to the bottom of the stairs. As I said, Mrs Fielding had gone into the room off the landing. My men were trying to get in."

"The door having been locked against them?"

"Yes."

"They were trying to kick this one down too?"

What promises to be a rise of laughter

is emasculated at once by the fierce sweep of the goatee.

"They had their shoulders to it. Then somehow the lamp got knocked off the table and burst and the flare-up caught the men's clothes, so they had to back off, beat the flames out."

"Did anyone think to call out to the woman, tell her what was happening?"

"Yes, Deputy Smith did. And I went out through the back way and around the side of the house to see if there was any way to get up there — and down. There wasn't."

"What then?"

"I ran back into the house. The fire had got a lot bigger. Everything was tinder-dry and caught hold real quick, the cloth from the table, the wallpaper."

"And your deputies? Where were your deputies?"

"Deputy Smith was just inside the front doorway. There was no sign of Deputy Cape. I went part of the way up the stairs. There was a lot of smoke and flame on the landing and around the stairs. I asked where Cape was. Smith said he'd already gone outside."

"So your own purpose in getting onto the stairs again was not solely to locate Deputy Cape?"

"No, it was to try to get to the room where the woman was. I shouted for Smith to leave and then tried to reach the landing but by that time the stairs were well afire. I got to maybe six steps short of the landing, which I couldn't see any more for smoke, and I had to back off. The fire had got into the roof fast and at that point some pieces of the ceiling started falling."

"The results," Whittaker observes, nodding to indicate the witness's gauze-swathed forearm, "are apparent." Whittaker's goatee dips as he looks down at his papers. He clears his throat. "I have viewed the remains of a female recovered from a fire which totally destroyed a house on Larchmont and I am satisfied that they are those of the occupant, one Bella Fielding, believed to be around thirty years of age and whose only known next-of-kin is Arnold John French of parts unknown. Cause of death asphyxiation as a result of the aforementioned house-fire, accidentally caused by law enforcement officers while pursuing their sworn duty. Witness is excused."

The tall man unwinds himself from where he has sat with scarcely a twitch of movement throughout, and is now seen to be wearing a pair of black pants tucked into the tops of plain, high-heeled half-boots, and he is carrying a battered, shallow-crowned black hat which he has done his best to make presentable but has plainly failed.

Pacing down the centre aisle, heels striking bare boards, he seems now unaware, or at least uncaring of the rows of blank, oval faces on either hand, of a near hundred pairs of eyes fastened on him. Apart from the footfalls of the tall man there are now no sounds whatsoever, not even an extraneous cough.

They might not be saying anything but doubtless they are thinking a lot and if the sum of all their thoughts in this long, crowded, airless room can be shaken down into one particular observation, it might well be:

"He'll have no need to go lookin' for Jack French no more. Ol' Jack, he'll come lookin' for him."

Some wishful thinking, perhaps, on the part of his critics, a simple churning behind the belt buckles of those who are, and always have been, deeply afraid of him.

It is true that from times past, in places other than this, certain of his exploits have passed into common currency: the determined hunting down of those who murderously hit the bank at Bridgewater, their bodies fetched back six days later across their own droop-headed horses, him leading them, bobbing out of the haze of a cool early morning, a solemn procession of the dead, a parade, a public display of dire retribution;

the facing down of the deserters, the murderous rapists Trooper Caine and Trooper Le Froy, run to ground just south of Bessemer's way-station in Fauls County; the sun-shafted evening fight in a stinking, weed-strewn street in a place called Nokes, one U.S. marshal dead, another dying, when, as the one man left standing, he came striding on inexorably towards Obe Wallace and the unspeakable Cato Wilkes and shot the both of them to bloodied rags, having closed to within ten feet of them at the end. And for each such event that could be recounted in detail, there are perhaps three or four others that are mere whispers on the wind, other times in other places.

He stalks these streets unchallenged.

The assembled citizens sit almost motionless for better than half a minute after his footfalls can be heard no more.

The deputies are the first to rise, to go walking together down the centre aisle, carrying old hats, looking at the floor.

2

HE was down off the wagon again, the second time inside an hour, gone off to one side in long, browning grass, hands on knees, vomiting in shuddering convulsions, though now a dangle of mucous was all there was to show for it.

An emaciated, once-tall individual, he was hatless and wearing faded Levis and a sand-coloured shirt which was hanging on his wasted frame.

The true age of this man would not have been easy to judge, for whatever the ailment was which clearly was ravaging him, it had caused his skin to tauten over his bones and to assume an appearance of yellowed parchment, and his eyes were deeply sunken in sockets resembling mere protuberances of bone. The skin of his neck had the corded aspect most often observed in the very old and his hands, reduced of substance, had developed an appearance of near transparency.

When the spasms which had been so sorely racking him had ceased, he remained for a little time in the hands-on-knees posture as though wary of straightening too soon lest another attack assail him.

The girl, a thin child of maybe no more than twelve, had remained up on the hide-covered wagon-seat and had wound the reins of the docile four-horse team around the brake-lever. Her whole attention, however, was on the narrow back of the man, waiting with an expressionless patience borne, perhaps, of long custom.

Her dress was yellow gingham with white collar and cuffs, a clean garment but one which had seen much wear and showed evidence of rubbing, even the beginnings of raggedness at all its extremities. Set together on the angled footboard were her small, well-worn boots, and between boots and the hem of her dress, dark wool stockings. On her head was a curl-brimmed, red felt hat devoid of decoration, and from beneath this, at the back, cascaded her thick, shining dark hair, reaching all the way down her small back. Her hands, clasped now in her lap, were slim and well formed, her neck was long and her oval face clean-skinned and of a dark cream complexion. The girl's brows were very thin and dark and her eyes were dark also and large, resembling those of a suspenseful little animal, but in their depths, sometimes, as now, lingered a deeper awareness of reality in an often unjust world than a child of her tender years might be expected to possess. It was, however, by no means evidence of hardness, merely the look of someone who tended to accept day-to-day occurrences for what they had come to be, rather than as she might have wished them to be; and the sicker the man became, the more introspective the child had become.

They had travelled some distance

to this point and still had a long way to go. "*Going to Kansas. To kin that's in Kansas.*" Last heard of in Kansas was something they chose, by some unspoken mutual agreement, not to add. And anyway, even between herself and her pa, '*Going to Kansas,*' was being mentioned less often now, maybe because their focus had come down to simply moving from one town to the next. *One town at a time*, the girl thought, might even have to be abandoned soon. Maybe there would be a doctor — a good doctor, not some posing barber — in the next one, but you could never be sure about that, not out here.

In back of her, beneath trooped canvas, were all the possessions they had been able to bring, not many, just enough to see them through the long journey northwards. And the man had some money with him, again not a great deal, but spread out over his figured time for the journey, sufficient to see them through. Maybe. Maybe not, now, since they had been compelled to slow to this faltering crawl.

Beneath the wagon-bed a spare wheel was slung, and water-casks were fixed on either side of the rig, and in a sturdy wooden box at the back were stored miscellaneous utensils and such food as they had elected to carry between towns and in case it became necessary to make an overnight camp.

Some places they had paused in longer than they had intended but that had been purely to do with the state of the man's health at the time, and it seemed to the young girl that another of these longer stop-overs would be coming up again real soon. It was plain that he was getting sicker, moving more slowly.

He was walking slowly. now, wiping his mouth and brow with a blue bandanna, coming back towards the wagon. When he was ready to climb back up, the girl extended one of her small hands and was able to help him a little with the last big effort needed for him to get up on the wagon-seat.

She saw that his eyes were watery and she could hear that his indrawn breaths were shaky and wheezing.

The girl unwound the reins and, grasping the lever with both hands, released the brake. She shook the long lines, yipped at the leaders and, harness jingling, the team began walking forward.

"You all right now, Pa?"

"Better, Immy. Better." The truth, she knew, was that he was far from all right, and *better* meant only that he was no longer on the point of vomiting.

Now, however, the girl gave her attention to driving the rig, keeping a look-out for any severe irregularities in the trail ahead, yet having to rely as much as anything on the good sense of the lead horses, while the man beside her, hang-headed, was grasping the edge of the seat with both his hands as though fearful that a lurch of the wagon might catch him unawares and send him pitching to the ground.

When they came crawling up a slight rise and beyond some juniper, the land, although still brush-scattered, lay more openly before them and suddenly against the white sky they saw the sharp angles of many roof-tops, smoke hanging above them like pale blue gauze.

No doubt this would be the sizeable town of Gabriel, perhaps a half-mile away, and as always when the haze of another town came into view the girl, though apparently preoccupied with her driving, was seized with conflicting emotions, some centred in the hope that here might be found more and better medication to ease her pa's condition, others around a fear that they might soon be confronted by some dire threat to their safety. She wanted and did not want to go rolling into a new, untried place where, right from the start, their progress would be marked by speculative eyes all the way up the main street, them and their much-travelled wagon and team, a man whose appearance suggested that he could not be long for this world and a skinny young girl who looked as though she ought to be in better care.

A couple of hundred yards short of Gabriel, beyond a clump of cottonwoods over to their left, some ramshackle buildings came into view; a house — or what remained of a house, for it appeared to be derelict — a barn and a cluster of greyish outbuildings, all afloat on a sea of stiff-moving grasses and tall weeds and with other trees close by.

It was when they were abreast of this sorry conglomeration that once again the man raised one of his bony hands to signal that he must get down off the wagon. So the girl hauled up firmly on the reins, leaning back on the seat, calling sharply to the leaders and then, as she had done a short time earlier, put both her hands to the brake-lever, this time to haul it on; she then wound

26

the leathers around it.

"Pa, you want me to help?"

He shook his head and climbed slowly down. This time, hands on knees, gasping and coughing, he could not produce even mucous, succeeding only in sweating profusely and draining his strength further, so that when eventually he made his way back to the wagon he was incapable of climbing onto it, even with the girl's help.

That was the reason for his making a weary half-gesture with one hand, indicating the huddle of weather-warped structures forty yards away, and for the man himself going quite slowly to the left, swishing through the long grass towards them.

Sadly the girl waited, watching the man's painful progress before she unwound the reins and prepared to follow him on the wagon.

Fully a quarter of an hour went by, him sitting on the nearly overgrown front stoop, before he recovered sufficiently to stand up and venture inside the old house to take a look around, the girl trailing him.

A couple of the rooms had taken overhead damage and the floors of those that were still sound were littered with debris from decaying inner walls. Three other rooms, however, one of them the big kitchen containing an iron stove, a long wooden table and four chairs and numerous drawers and cupboards, seemed generally sound enough, showing little evidence of assaults from weather apart from some staining.

"We'll have to hole up here for a few days, Immy, while I get some strength back. I've got to take some rest, away from the wagon." He was in pain again, too, she could tell, though he always tried to hide it.

"You need to see a doc again, Pa. Maybe there's one in this town, this . . . what is it?"

"Gabriel."

"Yeah . . . So I'll take the wagon on up there right now and find out."

Slowly he shook his head. "I don't want you going there alone, Immy."

"You've got to get some help."

The man regarded her out of his sunken eyes. Child she might be, but on occasions there was a certain confidence about her which he well knew had emerged as a direct result of their dire circumstances over these past months; and now hearing evidence of it again he had fresh doubts about the fairness and wisdom of his dragging her through all this when, with every day that went by, he was less able to function as he should. It was becoming increasingly unfair to the girl. And she needed schooling. Had they stayed where they were, say eight or nine weeks ago, and he had taken more care, he might have begun to get better. As soon as the thought came to him again, however — for it had come to him repeatedly in recent days — he dismissed it. Staying put had not been an option, and his daughter Imogen was the very reason for that. As he saw it he had but one chance to see the child to safety before, inevitably, he was overcome by the invasive disease that was consuming him, and that was by one determined effort, getting her up to Kansas to where her ma's kin were. To safety. Dully he did not wish to entertain the slightest doubt over it. *If they're still there. If they're willing to take her, to overlook all the disputes and acrimony, the taking of sides.* Those were matters he had been most reluctant to talk about with the child and now, as it had done before, it gave him a stab of guilt. Pain of another kind. To safety. Those were words that had other meanings, too, beyond the rightness of seeing to a young girl's welfare within what he hoped would be the warmth of family, and he had tried to avoid brooding over them while never losing sight of the fact that menaces were never far away and that his own defences had virtually gone. Yet, right from the start, he had said to the girl, "*We are who we are.*

We'll not hide it."

People were not slow to notice the wagon rolling by, the four-horse team being driven by a child who seemed scarcely robust enough for the task, glancing up from whatever they were doing, following the progress of this trail-dirty incoming rig.

What drew the girl towards the tall, big-shouldered man on the boardwalk was not so much the dulled badge on his black leather vest, but more the fact that standing alongside him was a boy of about her own age, with a round-brimmed black hat pushed to the back of his straw-coloured head and dressed in grey coveralls and a tan shirt; for the presence of this boy — at least in her estimation — seemed to diminish any threat there might have been from a man alone.

Only after she had hauled back on the reins and called to bring the team to a halt and had completed her two-handed act on the brake lever did the big man and the boy come to the edge of the boardwalk to stare across at the thin girl with her large eyes the colour of soot.

Solemnly, the man with the badge and who was dressed in black pants and a denim shirt under the black vest and was slung with a thickly-shelled gunbelt and a holster from which jutted a cedar-handled pistol, touched the brim of his shallow-crowned black hat and nodded to her.

"Ma'am." Then: "Come far?"

"Shearman." Her voice was not pipey but smooth and low-pitched and its tone seemed to embody its own story of an arduous journey. The girl was aware that the boy's striking cobalt eyes were fixed on her, unwinking and curious, but her attention was on the leathern face of the man. "I need to find a doctor right away, for my pa."

"Your pa's there in the wagon?" Concerned, the man made an involuntary move to go look.

At once the girl shook her head. "Back along the trail a ways there's a place — a house — kind of falling down. Pa got down off the wagon when he felt sick, then he couldn't get back up, so he's out at that place. Is there a doc here?"

"No." As soon as she heard it the girl's full lips parted and both the man and the boy could see a liquid brightness come into her dark eyes. "Gabriel's had no doc this year past, since the one that was here died. But there's a druggist in town, a good man. Mr. Likens." He shot a glance at the boy. "Rob, will you go let him know about this?" At once the boy left them to go jogging away up the main street, ignoring one or two people who were asking, "What's goin' on?" To the child the man repeated, "He's a good man, Mr Likens. He'll take a look at your pa, do what he can."

In what sounded like an attempt at justification she said, "There was nobody around up at that house."

"Nobody's been there for years. You'll not be disturbed." He did not

33

ask where they were headed in their wagon or why. "My name's Purnell. You or your pa need anything else, that office behind me is where I can be found. Or you could tell my son, Rob."

When word of these newcomers got around several of the women in Gabriel, Purnell's wife among them, were at once concerned, principally for the predicament of the girl.

"Up at Cavan's? They can't stay there. It's not fit."

Mary Purnell, Phena Crimond the wife of Gabriel's mayor, Mabel Hawtrey whose man owned the mercantile, the biggest enterprise in the town, and a few other women had been discussing it and they had agreed they would have to see what could be done, what better arrangements might be made.

At supper, Mary Purnell said, "Some of the women are going to look out for a more suitable place for that man and the child. From what I've heard, the poor mite looks like a good meal would knock her clear over."

"Her name's Imogen," the boy said.

His fair-haired mother turned to look at him. "How do you know that?"

"When I come back — "

"Came."

"When I came back from tellin' Mr Likens, she was still there, sittin' on the wagon. She told me then." Then he said, "They won't be stoppin' long in Gabriel anyway. They're on their way to Kansas."

"This is a mighty long way from Kansas," Purnell observed, "an' Vern Likens reckons that feller won't be going anywhere for some while yet."

"All the more reason to find a better place for them," his wife said. It seemed to have been assumed by the Gabriel women that wagon people were likely to have little money to spend on accommodation.

Purnell was eating steadily. It had been a long, rather tiring day and he had other matters on his mind which seemed to him more important than some ailing itinerant, though he himself had offered support of a kind to the child on the wagon, so he said, "Maybe I'll take a walk up there, have a talk with this man."

Mary Purnell regarded him out of cobalt eyes that were a match for those of her son. She was well aware of the pressures that were working upon him, the often fractious mood abroad in this place together with the real and immediate uncertainties now attending their own tenure here, the election not far off, Purnell having to tread a fine line, conscious of his vulnerability, which really meant the vulnerability of his small family.

Mary Purnell had long considered George Crimond and Henry Hawtrey to be chief among those who, in the playing of local politics, were making problems for Purnell, demanding of him what she was disposed to consider a great deal of service for relatively small reward. Yet upon reflection she had had to concede that perhaps it was really the nature of the town of Gabriel itself, its generally poor circumstances, which stood at the heart of all their problems. Times had not been good.

Men like Crimond and Hawtrey had invested in this town in the firm belief that the railroad would be bound to come through, but in the event it had not, nor did Gabriel get even a side-track. It remained served by a stage-line and was sustained, if at times tenuously, by cattle outfits, homesteaders down on the Lorient River and miners along its upper reaches.

Purnell watched his wife as she moved around clearing away dishes, then as she began pouring the coffee, said, "I do hear Abe Kettley is about to put his name up for marshal."

She straightened, coffee-pot in hand. "*Kettley?*" She did not need to say, "*George Crimond's brother-in-law?*"

"So I'm told."

"Who says so?"

He shrugged. "It's around town."

Pouring his coffee, she sighed, and he read her unspoken comment and added, "I'd give a lot just to tell 'em the hell with it, but there's no way we can afford to do that."

"If Kettley does stand, do you think there's a chance you might lose?"

"Maybe. But I reckon when it all shakes down I'll have the numbers, just, Crimond's brother-in-law or not."

During the next twenty-four hours, even the town's customary preoccupation with its own problems and the talk of coming elections was sidelined by general gossip about the sick man up at the old Cavan place and the young girl who was with him.

Then a passing rider, a ragged and bewhiskered man asking the way to the Diamond B, seeking, so he said, a range cook's job that he had vaguely heard about, also overheard talk of this wagon man and the girl.

"Sick feller, yuh say, with a girl along?"

"Yeah."

"This here girl, her name, would it be Imogen?"

"So the marshal's boy says."

The rider nodded, wiped a sleeve across his beaded nose, unhitched the sad-looking sorrel from McCurdie's tie-rail. "Yeah, wa-al, if that's the case I ain't sorry to be movin' on."

"What? How's that?"

"Cain't be two on 'em." He stood blinking at them. "Yuh ain't got yoursel's some run-o'-the-mill sick feller there, boys, not by a long chalk. What yuh got there is Charlie Troy hisself."

3

WORD of the coming of Charlie Troy had settled over all of Gabriel like a death-shroud and the piling up of dirty-looking cloud in the southwestern sky seemed like a fitting background for the mood that was now abroad.

Near the day's end Purnell came in looking tired and irritated and tossed his hat onto a chair and Mary, a single fine strand of her fair hair curled across a warm cheek, half turned from her tasks at the stove.

"Where's Rob?" Purnell asked.

"Upstairs. He'll soon be down though. Why?"

"I saw him with the Troy girl today."

"*With* her?"

Purnell rubbed one of his gnarled hands around his face, went across to the bubbling coffee-pot and poured himself a mugful.

"I mean he was talking with her. I saw her up near the bakery late this afternoon."

She was going on with what she was doing, but said, "What else happened?" She could feel the tension, knew that anger was not far below the surface and that probably it had nothing to do with their son or the girl.

"First George Crimond, then Henry Hawtrey — oh, an' some others as well. All of them asking the same question. What do I plan on doing about Charlie Troy."

She stood slowly wiping her hands on a small red and white checkered towel. "So what did you tell them?"

"I said as little as possible. But they have to understand that Troy isn't some felon. To my knowledge there's no such thing as a warrant out anywhere with his name on it; and by Vern Likens' account Troy's sick enough to have a problem moving anywhere right now. What do I do, load him on his wagon and give the team a whack?"

There was the sound of bumping down the stairs and the good-looking, fair-haired boy came in, and perhaps believing that it would sound less like an interrogation if it came from her, his mother said, "Pa tells me you saw the young girl from the wagon again today."

Guilelessly Rob Purnell's eyes shifted from mother to father. "Imogen. Yeah, we did talk some. She was up to the bakery an' then she was headin' along to talk with Mr Likens some more. I didn't see her after that. She says her pa's real sick."

Purnell had been about to ask if Imogen had mentioned how long they intended staying around Gabriel, then realized the absurdity of such a question in the circumstances, so instead he observed, "She's had to take a whole lot on, at her age, that's clear enough. Did she say anything else?"

"Nope. Well, not much."

"Best go wash up ready for supper," said Mary.

The boy went out.

Mary began lifting dishes down from the warming-rack above the stove and setting them out on a table that had been spread with a crisply-clean white cloth.

"I don't know much at all about this man Troy," she said, "just gossip, mostly, and most of that in the past few hours. Now everybody down the street wants to talk about him and most of them want him gone from here. Is even half of what they're saying about him true?"

"Probably not," Purnell said. "To my knowledge Charlie Troy hasn't been through here before this; but men like him do get to have a special kind of history. No matter where they go an' what they do, truth an' lies get tangled up. I've heard a lot about Charlie Troy over the years."

The boy had come quietly back in but was staying in the background.

43

"Wasn't he a lawman?" Mary asked. "Anyway, that's what Ellie Drucker was saying today. And he got into some kind of trouble."

"Yeah, he wore a badge, one time an' another," Purnell said. "An' I don't know what happened to his wife, where she went or when, or whether she's alive or dead. Left him with a child to take care of, whatever the reason." He sipped his coffee. "Lawman. A U.S. marshal once, too. All sorts of things. Brought up on a ranch in Wyoming, an' a real hard man in his day, Charlie; moved around with some hardnoses as well. Sometimes it's not that easy to draw the line between what's inside the law an' what's not, more particular if there's not much law around. Troy, he's been in land deals, speculation an' such. I've talked with men who've said Troy wasn't above lining his own pockets out of deals while he was on a county's payroll. But plenty of men in public office have to put up with that kind of rumour.

It's always hard to know how much of that kind of talk comes through envy or spite, fear even. But he sure got his name in the news a time or two. It was Charlie Troy that stuck like a damn' burr to three men that raided the Bridgewater bank an' fetched 'em all back six days later across their own saddles. An' Troy shot a pair of army deserters out of a dump somewhere south of Bessemer's — that's in Fauls County — where they'd been causing some havoc. Another time he went with other U.S. marshals after Ord Wallace an' Cato Wilkes, an' in the finish Troy was the only man left standing. People seem too ready to forget things like that, still want to paint a man like him black."

The boy could remain still no longer. "It was Mr Troy that shot Wilkes? Boy, everybody's heard about Wilkes, Pa."

Mary gave her son a glance that was faintly disapproving but his father said, "It was. Wilkes and Ord Wallace, both." Then to Mary, Purnell said, "But it was some business that concerned a man named Jack French that stirred things up the most. A few years back. A man who was wanted real bad, Jack French. Well, Troy was a county sheriff at the time, an' somehow he got word that French was at a house not much more than two hundred yards from the county jail itself, holed up, so he hit the place at night, Troy an' two deputies; but there was only a woman there, a Bella Fielding. French's cousin, she was, an' whatever happened after they busted in, a fire got started. Troy an' his men got out but the woman was burned to death."

"Brad, that's awful!"

"They do say Troy did his damndest to get to her an' got burned some himself while he was about it, but in the finish he had to, well, just back off an' make a run for it. The roof had started falling in. Some said he did do all he could. Some weren't so sure."

The boy had said not one word but

his eyes widened, hanging on every word and unnoticed.

Mary had paused in her tasks. "What happened over it?"

"There was an inquest. The fire was found to be an accident, so Troy an' his men were cleared of blame. But it was the beginning of the end for Troy as a county lawman, an' not long after that he moved away. I don't know where he went or what he did, but it must have been some good long while after, that he took ill."

"What happened about this man French?"

"I did hear he had the brass nerve to come seeking Troy but by then Charlie was gone, and the two deputies as well. It had got too unpleasant for those boys. No matter what a court said, they were seen to have saved themselves while a woman burned. Fair or not, that was the public verdict. They weren't so lucky, though, later. One, a man by the name of Cape, he was back-shot in some dump in New

Mexico, an' the other, Smith, he was found by cowmen on a range about a hundred and fifty miles from the town where the fire had been. Chained an' burned to death, swung across a fire."

One of Mary's hands crept to a cheek. "That's dreadful . . . inhuman. Was that done by Jack French?"

Purnell shrugged. "It was common knowledge that nobody harmed anyone connected with Jack French an' lived to tell about it. It's probably only a matter of time before he comes up with Troy. That's really why no town would be comfortable having Troy around. I've heard it's caused problems in other places. It's been said that having Troy in town is like having a plague, because sooner or later he'll bring death. Smaller fish than French, that wouldn't have dared swim in the same creek as Troy when he was in his prime, wanting a chance at him now that he can't fend for himself." Purnell smiled bleakly. "When that young girl turned up, even when she said she was looking for a doctor for her pa, it never even occurred to me that it was Charlie Troy. Maybe I'm losing my wits."

Mary was clearly shaken by what he had told her but she was again getting on with setting out the supper; yet she did say, "But the man is *ill*, very ill by all accounts. And there's the child . . . They mustn't just be driven out onto the trail. It would be inhuman."

"Well, I didn't say I'd do it."

She glanced over her shoulder. "Mightn't you be forced into it?" She was under no illusion about the awkward corner that Purnell now seemed to have been pushed into.

"We'll see." It was as though he wanted to thrust the problem away, at least for a while.

When supper was over and the boy had gone up to his bed, Mary Purnell spoke more openly, her concern showing markedly now, for the strain of the new threat of Abe Kettley angling for the town marshal's post had brought with it a host of uncertainties.

"It could mean we'd have to move on, Brad, leave Gabriel. Where could we go?"

"Let's worry about that only if we have to," he said. "But if this argument over Troy, about the man being allowed to stay here, gets worse, it could make a difference."

"Well, the women here won't let that child come to any harm, whatever else happens." As soon as she had said it she wondered if that were strictly true. Some of them had been concerned about the young girl as soon as they had heard about her. Yet this town had always been influenced by what its menfolk deemed should be done; so if the men should decide now what was to be done, the compassion of the women might swiftly evaporate. This very day Mary, talking with Mabel Hawtrey and Phena Crimond, believed she sensed already some slight hesitations. Or had she imagined it? She felt confused. Now, however, she said, "Annie Walenski stopped me in the

street to ask about the Troy child."
Plain Annie, the Gabriel schoolteacher, darned and dowdy, struggling on in a none-too-salubrious back room at the old Ganley store-house, with a pot-bellied stove, a long blackboard, some desks and hard chairs; but all that this town had to offer as a school.

Yet Annie Walenski had always refused to be deterred, she herself beyond the age now, it was assumed, for a schoolteacher's escape into matrimony. She got $35 a month plus cheap lodgings with the Mulvaney family. And school was taught in Gabriel eight months of the year rather than the five or six common to many like places across the western lands. "She wanted to know how long they were going to be here, and about getting the little girl to school. She thought I might know something."

Purnell had to smile slightly. "Annie never likes to miss out on a new one anywhere inside thirty miles. Well, how long, that's something nobody knows yet. If I do go up there to have a word with Troy, maybe I'll ask him about the school."

"You will go?" Purnell knew that she was genuinely anxious about the Troys situation. To be so was a manifestation of her nature in regard to the misfortunes of others. Yet as always she stopped short of encroaching on what she acknowledged as his preserve, all those matters to do with his job here as town marshal.

"Probably. Hawtrey in particular isn't likely to let this go now that the talk's started, so I guess I'll need to go see for myself what kind of state Charlie Troy is in. I'll need to have the facts. Then we'll see."

Softly, Mary said, "Hawtrey." She did not like the stringy, lard-faced man down at the mercantile, and occasionally had had trouble concealing that fact.

Also, there was something amiss between Hawtrey and his softly-spoken, mousey little wife, Mabel. Pain was there somewhere, Mary felt certain, yet although she had been on good terms with Mabel Hawtrey for as long as she had been in Gabriel, not one word of discontent had come from the woman; though Mary thought there had been times when Mabel had been on the brink of saying something, but at the last moment had held back. Mary wondered if Mabel's reticence had been through reasons of marital loyalty or perhaps through fear. Be that as it may, Henry Hawtrey exercised real influence in this town and was by no means a man to cross.

"Like the man or not," said Purnell, knowing what was in her mind, "he's a man who could cause problems if it suited him. For Charlie Troy. For us."

"What *would* suit him," she said, "would be to see Abe Kettley installed in the marshal's office. And we've said it often enough before, George Crimond might be elected mayor but it's Hawtrey who pulls a lot of the strings." Mary would by no means have been alone in such a belief, for the moon-faced George Crimond who operated a dozen freight-wagons, astute enough when it was a matter of protecting his personal fortunes, was often seen to be too readily influenced by Henry Hawtrey who, as it happened, was not even a member of the seven-man town council. What Mary Purnell had not said, perhaps because she had felt unsure of Purnell's reaction was: *"And I've never liked the way he looks at me."*

The conversation then moved on from Hawtrey and Crimond, for those men were not the only ones who had been of concern to Purnell over recent hours.

"Ed Voller's in town, been hanging around up at Cole's livery an' at the Longhorn. Ed must've got his hands on some coin somewhere."

"One day that man is going to make real problems for you, Brad."

"An' one day somebody's going to

catch him in the act of laying his iron to beef that's not his," observed Purnell dourly, "an' save me the task."

An unwashed, raggy man, Voller, who came and went, a man in his early forties, addicted to the shot-glass, and who owned a badly run-down cattle outfit some twenty miles to the north-east of Gabriel. Not above theft, Ed Voller, so Purnell had long believed, and a compulsive braggart. Slung with an old Forehand and Wadsworth .44, he was disposed to talk big when the drink was in him, rumoured to have shot a man dead, years ago, in a saloon in Butte, Montana. Some of Cad Walsh's Tall W riders drank with Voller and were, in Purnell's opinion, no better specimens than Voller; and when they all came together in one of the saloons, intimidated citizens had been known to come seeking Purnell to take a hand. A Wells Fargo guard who had knowledge of Voller in his Montana days had proffered advice to Purnell: *"Never turn your back on that bastard. An' watch him around the girls.*"

Mary glanced up as the first raindrops began beating against the window and gave a slight shudder. Purnell noticed.

"What's the matter?"

"Nothing . . . Oh, I don't know, Brad. I've just got a bad feeling, half scared." again: "I don't know."

"Is it all about Charlie Troy?"

She moved closer to the dark window, seeing her own reflection in the rain-flecked pane and Purnell's gaunt, hard face in the lamplit room behind her.

"Maybe. Hawtrey, Crimond, this whole sorry place. The undercurrents." She turned to look at him and he could see the trouble reflected in her eyes. "Brad, Vern Likens might well have been down to see this man Troy, but it's not enough."

"I've said I'll go."

"Then let me come with you. There might be something I could do."

He drew a slow breath, scraped at

his now stubbled jaw.

"It's maybe best you don't get involved in this, Mary."

"With the child, you mean? How old is she? Eleven? Twelve? I don't know whether the other women will try to help or not, in the finish, but I'll not wait to find out."

"If you go they might not understand, Mabel, Phena, the others."

"Right at the start they were all concerned over Imogen in particular, but today they were almost, well, backing off. But nothing said outright of course."

"I think it best I go down there on my own, Mary. If anything should start to fly back, I wouldn't want to see it flying back in your face."

She stood rubbing her long fingers together slowly. "All right. Don't forget to ask about the school, for Annie." Then: "I'm tired, Brad. I'm going to bed."

Left alone, the stove now burned low, more rain pattering against the window,

Purnell felt a sudden wave of unease pass through him as though some small hint of the violence sometimes said to be attracted by Charlie Troy had actually begun to infect him.

4

FOR all Purnell knew pain might have been spearing the man but here in the light of a low lamp and in the fading rouge glow of an iron stove, Troy claimed to be *"Better. Better than when we got here."*

That same night after his conversation with Mary, Purnell had made his way to the Cavan place, wanting to settle certain matters in his mind, preferring darkness, risking . . . risking he knew not what, to get close to Charlie Troy, to talk a while with the man, the child sleeping, presumably, in a nearby room; one of the rooms which still had enough of a roof over it to keep the rain out.

Troy was mobile, slowly, deliberately so, but soon after Purnell arrived, retreated to an ancient, torn, hide-covered chair in a kitchen redolent of cooked food, and slumped back with a small hiss of relief, and sat for a time drawing in restoring breaths; then in a surprisingly firm, though quite low voice, he said:

"So you're Purnell. I thought you'd show up sooner or later. My girl Imogen, she's told me about you."

Rain was sounding on the roof.

"Yeah, I'm Purnell, the sworn law in Gabriel."

"Well," Troy said, "I can see you're an after-dark marshal, which could mean one of two things." He paused, drawing in further long breaths as though each word might be causing him some discomfort. "You're here to do what, up to now, nobody else has managed to get done, anywhere, or you want to cover your own ass 'til you find out what's what." Troy looked down a moment as though summoning more strength. Then: "I'll have to make a hopeful throw of the dice an' say it's the second one."

"That's about it," Purnell said. "And

I took a chance you'd still be awake."

"I don't get a whole lot of sleep nowadays." He made a small gesture. "There's coffee in the pot over yonder. We've got the basics here." When Purnell shook his head, Troy asked, "Who's place is this? Somebody in town? So far I've seen no claimants."

"No," said Purnell. "Those that built this were before my time, an' they're long gone, so I was told when I came here. No kin have ever come to claim it. Sometime, if it doesn't rot first, maybe the county will move on it."

"Yeah, well. But that's not the main problem, is it, Purnell?" Troy moved slightly in the capacious chair as though a comfortable posture was no longer possible for any length of time, and when the poor light caught him afresh, Purnell could see more clearly the fragile thinness, the bone-thrusting state of the man, with his vellum-like skin and his dark eyes buried deep in sockets that were like shadowed caverns; and because of the tautness of his facial skin, Troy's almost bloodless lips were beginning to be forced slightly apart exposing a rim of upper teeth in what was a rictus of disease and continual pain.

"No," conceded Purnell, "you're right, Charlie, that's not the main problem here. No, it's the sound of your name, that brings with it all kinds of alarms, just like somebody's come out to hammer on swinging iron, fetching 'em all to their windows. It's a name that sure cuts through all the talk, is Charlie Troy."

"Well," said Troy again shifting around awkwardly in the chair, at the same time emitting a slight gasp, "one time there might've been good enough reason for that, the way things were, all the things that went on. We had our problems, an' one or two of 'em had to be shot, because there was just nothing else for it. But, by God, that was a hell of a time back. A whole lot's happened since then." He gave another slight gasp and this time held his ribs.

"But it's not really Charlie Troy on his own that bothers your friends in town, is it?"

"Not entirely," Purnell agreed.

"No," Troy said, "it's all about what blowflies Charlie Troy might fetch here if he's allowed to hang around, if he fails to move on, an' take his disease away with him."

Purnell nodded. "That's about it." Then: "Vern Likens — he's been?"

"Yeah." Troy nodded, blinking soporifically. "A good man, Likens, I reckon. Even better, because he fetched morphine." When Purnell said nothing to that, Troy went on, "Anyway, from where *I* sit, all this is not about me, it's about Imogen. She's twelve years old, Purnell, an' apart from some of her ma's kin that I hope to locate up in Kansas, there's nobody else for her. Up around Junction City." The wasted man took another deep breath. "No way is it my wish to stay around this town or any other. I have to keep rolling, for I reckon it'll be a close enough thing whether the trail runs out first, or I do. An' I've got about enough coin to get us where we're going, an' a bit over, so Immy won't be beholden. I can't afford to use up much more of it in places like Gabriel."

"I can understand that," Purnell said, "but I'd say you're in no shape to move anywhere for a while. That what Vern Likens said to you?"

Troy nodded wearily. He said then, "I can't blame the people here. God knows what they're afraid of is real enough, but there's not a lot I can do about it, not yet awhile. An' the men that might come, well, there'd be something to be got out of nailing a man like me. You know it, I know it. An' it's been tried already, on this journey." When Purnell's eyebrows were raised. Troy said, "In a dump called Charlotte, for one, an' in another, Caber's Ferry. Oh, they were third-raters, both, an' it so happened I was moving somewhat better, then. An' I still had the pistol.

I didn't cause either of those boys any permanent grief, but there was something of a dust-up, both times. The citizenry wanted me gone, of course, an' no argument. In Caber's Ferry I got the pipe-end of a 10-gauge poked in one ear to kinda make the point."

At what resembled a faint mewing sound Troy turned his cadaverous face, then relaxed, his head subsiding. Only the child in her adjoining room, stirring in her sleep.

"Still had the pistol." Purnell's attention had fastened on that.

"We had to get out of there in a real hurry, I couldn't get back to where we'd been sleeping, so in all that, some stuff got left behind. I couldn't risk Imogen. Belt, pistol, ammunition, all left." He paused, filling yellowed cheeks, blowing a breath out. "Peacemaker. I'd had it by me a good long while." Troy made a small movement that could have been a shrug. "So now here I sit, marshal, naked to every goddam' wind that blows."

Purnell nodded slowly and said, "As far as eviction from here is concerned, if certain men in Gabriel do start pushing the point, it'll still be me that has to do it. So, pistol or no pistol — an' that's something best kept between us — rest easy. But I have to say it wouldn't help if some other bastard did turn up, third-rater or not, an' drop the fat in the fire."

Troy, face shadowed, stared at Purnell, weighing what he had said. "I'm obliged to you."

Purnell said then, "My wife wants to come here, help your girl out, do what she can to ease things."

"From what you've told me tonight, that wouldn't win her no favours."

"Mary's never been one to look for favours. We'll see, but don't be surprised if a fair-haired woman comes knocking."

The sound of rain on the roof had diminished but now came back with a brief rush.

"One woman's been here already," said Troy. Again he shifted stiffly in his chair. "Annie Wal-something. Skinny woman, middle-aged. Said she was the school-teacher."

"Annie Walenski," said Purnell. "Come recruiting, no doubt."

"Yeah," said Purnell, "an' she took a good look around an' didn't miss much. About the school, I told her we'll see. All depends on how long we need to stay. Imogen sure wants to go to the school. I want her to go. She's missed far too much on account of me. It's been real hard on her. If we can't get back on the trail for a few weeks, she'll go to the classes."

"My boy, Rob, he'll watch out for her."

"So she says," said Troy. "So she says." Purnell thought that Troy almost smiled. "Kids can get a lot of things done fast, an' few questions asked."

"This town," said Purnell, "is no different to a lot of others. There's some good folks here but from time to time the wrong kind of men are around. The townsmen themselves, the ones that count, they're beset with a mixture of self-interest an' fear. But the ripples about Charlie Troy are bound to have spread out well beyond Gabriel."

Troy sighed, a drawn-out, hissing sound between his teeth. "If any of the scum do come here, well, they come," he said, "for there's no more I can do about that now." And once again he said, "Imogen, she's all that matters to me, getting her to Kansas before this grinding shit of a thing I've got stops me in my tracks for good an' all."

"Just be on your guard," Purnell said, knowing as soon as he had said it how absurd it must have sounded. But then he said, "Right now the town's real nervy. There's a kind of fear around, no doubt. It's in the air. I can smell it, even see it sometimes."

Purnell stood up and moved across to the window. There was no shade to pull down but a raggy curtain remained, and this he drew across to more or less screen the rain-speckled glass.

"You want that lamp left burning?"

"No," said Troy.

Purnell moved to it and turned it all the way down, then without another word went out into the rain, leaving the dying man in near-darkness, only the faintest of rose glows now showing in the stove.

The child's sleep was attended by phantoms. Vaguest of all, eternally beyond her reach, her mother. Even awake, Imogen could not remember her, no detail whatsoever of her appearance. Nothing had survived save perhaps perfume. Sometimes, if the girl smelled lilac-water, there was an immediate following thought — no, barely a thought — of her mother, but never was there a face that would come into view. In dreams, her father's face was always strong and clear; never was it the sick face, always the face as it had been before.

Sleeping, or even in drowsy wakefulness, sometimes she regained too, an impression of flickering lights moving across a stained ceiling in a room somewhere, and as soon as it came to her she would be brought abruptly to total wakefulness, filled with apprehensions whose source she was never able to identify; but it all had to do, she thought, with some kind of fire.

But other images sufficient to bring her awake in the dark had their origins in scenes that had been shockingly real to her. No matter that her dreams of them now were soundless, there were flickers of gunflame and men with wild eyes, running; and starting awake from these, was often to discover her pa there, his long arms enfolding her. *"Immy . . . Immy . . . It's all right. There's nothing, no-one else here. There's only you an' me . . . "* Her pa, with the soft gleam of thick new shells all around his belt, and the clean, curved butt of the great pistol, the Peacemaker.

She came half awake now, fancying that there had been voices and the closing of a door; then listening, heard only rain beating on the roof.

A woman in a rusty blue dress, an old coat and a black, unadorned straw hat had come today, afoot, not long after Mr Likens' buggy had gone bumping away, a long-faced but not unkindly woman named Walenski, a school-teacher, and her father, better in health than he had been a few hours before, but still far from fit to travel, had said, *"We'll see."* The thought of walking up to Gabriel to a schoolroom of strangers' faces filled her with doubts, yet she wanted desperately to go, even if it turned out to be only for a couple of weeks. Anyway, she already knew Rob Purnell. The fair-haired boy with his steady, open gaze and his quiet voice had accepted her situation unhesitatingly, as though there was nothing at all unusual about it, and that had surprised and pleased her, though she had not shown it.

She turned on her side and closed her eyes. She would see how her pa felt tomorrow, maybe talk to him about the school.

In all of Gabriel on this unpleasant night, few lamps were shining. A hunched figure in a slicker went hastening away across a dark yard, splashing through puddles, a yard in back of a grain-store, Little's, and under a poled awning there, watching the man departing, Voller stood sheltering from the rain, the raw spirit that he had been drinking not quite conquering the chill of the night or the foulness of his breath.

So, it was true, what he had been told elsewhere, Charlie Troy was here, sheltering too, in his fashion, up at Cavan's. Well, hell. Voller, his lumpy, stubble-whiskered face screwed into a grimace of distaste, peered up at the moving sky wondering if the rain was indeed easing. Then it occurred to him that maybe Cam Hackman was still sitting in on a game in Seifert's back room. If he was, then what better time to draw him aside to impart this piece of news.

Voller settled his wet hat more firmly on his head and went tramping away through the dripping dark.

5

THESE were no phantoms.

Imogen started from sleep, rising from her bedroll, the chill of the morning striking at her, and bare-footed, went first to the window, then softly into the next room.

In the old, hide-covered chair her father was sleeping, still fully dressed, his pitifully bony face cast down against his shrunken chest, his breathing wheezily audible but steady, and she now moved across to the window in this room, not wishing to disturb him, for nowadays he slept so seldom because of pain; this particular rest, however, perhaps induced by Likens.

A tattered curtain had been pulled across the window and she drew this aside, peering out into the damp, clouded-over early morning, across a weed-strewn yard among desolate, tumbledown outbuildings, but could see no-one.

She had heard horses, of that she was certain, not horses being ridden urgently, merely loping along, blowing, their bit-chains clinking; no voices, only the sounds of the horses. And they had neither come closer nor gone further away, as though the riders — for without a doubt there was more than one — were for some reason circling these buildings.

Imogen allowed the remnant of curtain to fall back and turned her head. Her father had not stirred. On her small, narrow feet, she left the room and visited each of the undamaged rooms in turn, going to the windows, trying to see through dirt-stained glass where glass remained, clasping herself against the cold. She could still hear the movements of the horses but though she looked most carefully, could see nothing stirring out there, perhaps because of poor light and the unruly clumps of brush and the dripping trees.

There was a relatively open place at the front where the trail to Gabriel passed by, but whoever these riders were they could not have been making a complete circuit, for though she made herself wait, they did not pass across that space. Again she went softly from window to window, pausing at each, watching and listening until eventually she came to realize that all sounds out there had ceased.

The girl, in her short lifetime, had smelled the special rankness of fear before, and every fibre of her being was alive with it now. Back in the kitchen she allowed the curtain to fall and turned away to see the man's deeply-sunken eyes as black as midnight, black as her own were, open, looking at her.

"What is it, Immy?" His voice was husky, strained, and he had not moved a muscle.

The child had no thought of deceiving him in some bid to save him anxiety, for his own dictum for survival was burned deeply into all her waking hours. "*Hide nothing. Say what's troubling you. It could mean the difference between life and death. For both of us.*" The man himself had maybe considered it an unfair burden for a young girl, but thought, equally, that he had no option.

"I heard horses, Pa, but there's no sounds now." She had not said *they've gone*, for she did not know whether or not that was the case. When it seemed that he might come struggling up out of the chair she shook her head quickly. "I've been all around a couple of times. They didn't come close, and I couldn't see anything." She turned away, a pale, skinny ghost in her nightdress in the dimness of the room. "I'll go get dressed now, Pa, and light the stove."

Today was the day she was to go up to Annie Walenski, to the school, but now she was no longer sure that she wanted to go anywhere, leaving her pa here alone. It was an absurd protective instinct. She would have been incapable of putting any defence into practice, but she felt the compulsion none the less.

* * *

Sometime during the early-morning hours the rain had ceased, but the sky of the new day was still the colour of gunmetal, and all things in Gabriel, according to their nature, had acquired the dullness or the brightness that the overnight rain had brought to them.

Main had become no more than a corridor of rutted yellow mud slurried by the passage of wheels and of horses, and everything and everyone passing along it became spattered and stained with it. The smell of mud and dung and dampness was everywhere, overlaid by the penetrating tang of chimney-smoke which, in faint airs coming out of the south, was being stranded across the roof-tops. The atmosphere was cold, and all who ventured out had coated themselves heavily against it.

Three women stood on the boardwalk beneath an awning outside Vern Likens' drugstore, Phena Crimond, Mabel Hawtrey and Mary Purnell, Mary in her deep purple, hooded cloak, the other two in long dark coats and black bonnets, as though they might have dressed deliberately to match the sombre cast of the day.

They had met here by chance, but now, and with some dismay, Mary Purnell had come to believe that it was an encounter which was causing Phena Crimond in particular a discomfort which was foreign to her nature, as though, had she seen the opportunity early enough, she would have avoided meeting Mary altogether. Today, neither of them seemed at all willing to talk any more about the Troys, but Mary could not simply allow the matter to lapse, and said:

"I've made up my mind. I'm going up there today, to Cavan's, to find out if there's anything at all that can be done for them. If there is, can I still count on you?"

"Well I do worry about that child," Mabel Hawtrey said, "but of course, that man . . . " She trailed off in some slight confusion.

"That man," Mary said, "is desperately ill." It was all she could do to hold back from saying it sharply.

Then Phena Crimond, as though from some rag-bag of talk and opinion she had found elsewhere, blurted out, "Mary, it's *who* he is." As soon as she had said it, however, she seemed to regret having spoken and half turned her head away.

Mary looked at her more closely and now noticed that today Phena was wearing more face-powder than usually she did, making her naturally pale face seem even paler, and the sickly-sweet smell of the stuff was noticeable. The woman obviously did not want to meet Mary's eyes and glanced down.

Mary said then, "My husband's been down there already. Brad's seen for himself the way things are and he's convinced the man isn't fit to move anywhere, not yet anyway; and I'm sure that's what Mr Likens would say, too. In fact he *has* said so."

The man himself, Likens, wearing his short white coat, was moving around inside his store just behind them, a vague shape beyond the steamy window. Suddenly Mary felt she would have been much relieved if the grey-haired, calm druggist who was not a man to be influenced readily by popular talk, had come out to confirm what she had said, but of course he was out of earshot.

"Naturally, Mary, we'll do whatever we can, in the circumstances," Mabel Hawtrey said then, but it sounded like only the first half of a statement, one which had nearly carried some kind of qualification. It was yet another signal, Mary thought, that they had been discussing Troy at length and had decided to do nothing — or had had that decision made *for* them. Hawtrey's lean, sour face came to her mind.

Along the street, over Mabel Hawtrey's shoulder and some forty yards away, two men had come wandering out of the mercantile and were standing now under its awning, deep in conversation, the long-nosed, raw-faced Hawtrey himself and a thickly-coated, stocky man wearing a brown derby; this was the Gabriel mayor, George Crimond, a man with a round, soft face and doe-like eyes, an almost obsequious individual, yet a man in whose presence Mary Purnell had never felt quite comfortable. There was something that was not quite right about George Crimond, but try as she might, she had never been able to pin-point what it was.

A third man had now joined these two outside the mercantile, a thin, somewhat spidery individual who Mary recognized, though at this time a narrow-brimmed eastern-style hat was covering his almost completely bald head; this was Abe Kettley, the brother-in-law of George Crimond and the man who, so she had heard, would be standing in the election against Brad Purnell for the job of town marshal. That was something that was still not easy to believe.

Mabel Hawtrey, like Phena Crimond, her back towards the mercantile, now sensing Mary's deep disappointment after what had been said at the outset, thought perhaps to make amends.

"I'll tell you what I'll do, Mary, I'll look out some fabric. Maybe we could all make up some dresses for the child. And a coat, perhaps."

"Imogen," Mary said.

"Yes . . . Imogen . . ."

"I could . . . Yes, I could easily do some of the sewing," said Phena Crimond, but in a reduced voice as though she believed that if she did not say it out too loudly, then she might not be irrevocably committed to do anything.

"I expect it will be a start," said Mary.

But then Mabel said, "Mary, do you still think it's *wise* to go up there yourself? I mean, as we've said, we could all do something for the — for Imogen, anyway, and — "

"The man — Imogen's father — is not some kind of ogre," Mary said. "He is a one-time lawman, once even a U.S. marshal, who is now very ill and who has a young daughter totally dependent on him, and for the present he's in too bad a shape even to look after her properly. She's trying to look after *him*."

"A one-time lawman maybe, Mary, but a whole lot of other things besides, or so I've been told," murmured Phena Crimond. There could be no doubt, Mary thought, where that had come from.

Mary looked sadly at the little woman. This meeting today was not with the Phena she knew, the relentlessly cheerful woman, always ready to offer help to those whom she believed needed it, the busy wife of the mayor of Gabriel.

Then Mabel Hawtrey, half turning, suddenly noticed the men who had gathered under the awning up at the mercantile and in a quick, involuntary movement, touched Phena on the arm.

Mary thought that Phena almost jumped with shock when she realized not only that the men were there but that the attention of all three was now fixed upon the group of women who were standing talking outside the drugstore.

Afterwards, to Purnell, Mary said, "It was as though they'd both been burned. They couldn't get on their way fast enough. *So many things to do.*" And when Purnell, a touch wearily, gently nodded his understanding, what amounted to his resignation over what he had been told, Mary added, "Phena, in particular though, was *different*, right from the start. It bothered me. All the good-humour was missing, as though it had been drained away. Or struck away." When his gaze turned quizzical she said, "She had put a lot of powder on her face. Too much, I thought. But one time when she turned her head to one side, I'm quite sure, Brad, that it must have been there to cover a bruise on her cheekbone."

★ ★ ★

Imogen had on a brown dress with darker brown figuring, a garment that had seen better days and might well have been cut down from a dress that was once the wear of a very small woman. She had arrived, cold, outside the back door at Ganley's empty storehouse on one of the side-streets off Main, there to enter the room which Annie Walenski used as a school.

It was a place of dull walls and dull, damp clothing, of inbred dowdiness and old boots. A long blackboard had been fixed to one wall; there was a pot-bellied stove with a blackened flue, some very old desks and small, hard chairs which might have been acquisitions from some abandoned school-house elsewhere, the seats polished from use, the desks scored and initialled.

Annie Walenski in her sombre blues and black, her long, lined face and her raw knuckles, smiled at Imogen and gave her a stub of pencil and a small notebook with a few unused pages at the back, and showed her where she was to sit, all under the curious scrutiny of two dozen girls and boys whose ages must have ranged from seven to thirteen, some of them wide-eyed, wet lips hanging open to the newcomer, some foxy and suspicious, one or two of them surly, their minds already made up about her. Rob Purnell sat at a desk towards the back but he had not looked directly at the girl nor she at him.

Annie Walenski required Imogen to stand and give her own introduction.

"My name is Imogen Marion Troy and I am twelve years old and I was born in San Antonio, Texas."

If any of them had expected her to whisper, to be coyly hesitant, then they would have been disappointed. She had provided them with no opportunity for sniggering. She stood straight, very thin in her old-fashioned dress, her skin quite pale and very smooth, her small ears seeming almost transparent, her rich, dark hair centre-parted, secured at the back of her neck with a scrap of brown velvet, falling to the out-curve of her bottom. Her very large, sooty eyes were frank but not bold and there was a calmness about them — something she did not necessarily feel — that caused Annie Walenski to visualize immediately a child who had had to see too much and hear too much of adult things during her short life, and was therefore no longer likely to be very much surprised by anything. At once it seemed to set her apart and for the first time Annie was concerned about that. As far as some of her pupils were concerned — and some of their elders — it was by no means seen as an advantage to appear to be in any way different from the dull run of humanity. It engendered suspicion and in the end, enmity.

That was quick enough to surface. It occurred at the lunch-time recess when Imogen left the classroom and set out to walk back down to where her pa was. She intended to fix him a meal, if indeed he would take any food, before afternoon school, for Annie Walenski was not content to be a mornings-only teacher and had made that clear to Imogen. *"Back here sharp at one."*

When she came along the alley, going towards Main, a lanky, cast-eyed boy wearing knickerbockers, and whose name was Dave Schiller, stood in Imogen's path.

"So, your name's Troy."

"My name is Imogen."

"Your name's a whole lot worse'n that around here. In fact, in Gabriel, your name's horse-shit."

The girl was aware that other children were filing out of the room, constrained

89

by Annie's '*Walk out!*' There was no sign yet of Rob Purnell, but now there was Annie Walenski's long face at the doorway.

"David Schiller . . . stop blocking the doorway! Go on . . . go!"

Russet-faced, resentful, he turned and went scuffing along the damp alley.

Though the outside chill was biting at her through her thin dress Imogen waited for him to pass from sight before she herself went hurrying away, arms crossed in front of her, hands clasped to her shoulders.

★ ★ ★

With an insight which should not have surprised her the bone-man in his strained, husky voice, said again, "They'll none of 'em look kindly on you when they get to hear about this."

Mary Purnell, some of the work now behind her, paused to glance at him. Troy had demonstrated that he was capable of moving around, performing small tasks which extended to fetching in wood for the stove, taking his time, fossicking in sheltered areas for fuel that was reasonably dry; but it was equally plain that he tired quickly and he had to rest often, sometimes declining to sit, but instead, standing, holding onto the back of the old hide chair for support.

At first she had been shocked by his appearance but she had managed to keep from showing it, setting out the cans and jars and bowls she had brought with her in a deep cane basket, and had set about tidying and wiping clean all the kitchen surfaces. When she had finished this she felt that, even so, she had not managed to make much of an impression on this desolate place, but it was the best she had been able to achieve in the time. Discarded clothing — though there was little of it — she put into a basket to be taken away for laundering.

The stove aglow, the coffee-pot

bubbling, and Mary, her face slightly flushed, a strand or two of her fair hair wisping across her forehead, was now about ready to leave, promising, however, to return.

"They can look on me how they want, Mr Troy."

Perhaps something in the way she said it, though, struck a different chord in the beleaguered but still alert man who stood gripping the chair and studying her. She was indeed a good-looking woman.

"They could harm you. They could harm you in other ways. Through your husband, maybe, or your son."

Mary flicked him an almost startled look. Troy could hardly have known of the worrying business of the election for marshal, for Purnell would have been unlikely to have talked about that when he had been here. She realized then that this was not information he was recalling but came of instinct; instinct for deceit and prejudice and fear, of knowing how people were, and of a deep understanding of human vulnerability.

"What will be will be." It sounded so hollow, even to her, yet her tone was firm when she said again, "I'll be back."

She put on her purple, hooded cloak and left him then, making mental note of things to be done next time. There had been no evidence of wet-weather clothing, and she believed that Imogen might not have any. That must be put right as soon as possible. She hurried on, back towards the smoke-misted shapes of Gabriel and could not have known that other, malevolent eyes were following her.

* * *

Dave Schiller had acquired allies, two of them, a plump, unkempt boy of perhaps ten, and another red-headed, squinty one wearing brown pants with faded knees, and about Imogen's own age. They kind of herded her into a yard off the alley moments after school was out that afternoon and it had all the earmarks of a premeditated move.

"Troy," Schiller said, pushing at her, setting her stepping backwards. "Whatever-your-damn'-name-was Troy. Yuh got to understand yuh ain't *wanted* here. Everybody's sayin' it. So why don't you an' that half-dead pa yuh got git gone from Gabriel afore all the scum there is comes here lookin' for him?"

Going by, Rob Purnell glanced in, then stopped and said to Schiller, "Back off her, Dave. Let her be."

"Ah. Purnell. So who yuh gonna be today? The marshal's li'l deputy?"

The plump boy and the red-headed one sniggered but stepped away, for Rob had now come right inside the yard. Schiller looked fit to spit iron but the others had gone quiet and there was a flicker of something else in Schiller's yellow eyes and he and Rob Purnell fell to arguing, no blows struck, the others backing further off, watching, hoping perhaps for a fight, which in the event never began.

When, eventually, Rob Purnell turned away, Imogen had already vanished. At the alley's mouth, standing under an awning on Main, for the light rain was falling again, he looked in vain for some sight of her. (From that day on, however, Imogen would wait silently for him when school came out, and without any evidence of surprise, he would walk with her almost as far as the Cavan place, saying little, hands in pockets, kicking at mud as he went.) Rob Purnell knew however that more trouble would be bound to come out of the encounter today, and in this he was right. Yet he did not know, at least to begin with, that Dave Schiller was only a part of the reason she waited to walk with him, that she harboured much more substantial fears.

The embarrassing, heart-beating moment of being pushed into the yard, the cruel, skewed eyes of the boy, were still in Imogen's thoughts as she went hurrying, with dampening hair, down the rough trail, even pushing aside the delight she had felt, earlier, coming back at noontime, to discover that Mrs Purnell had been there and had done housework, had brought food and had prepared a meal, had taken clothing away to be laundered. The effect on her pa had been plain to see.

She did not know the man was near until he stepped from concealing brush and took her by one arm and certainly she did not know that his name was Ed Voller, a dirty man with studded leather leggings and stained grey shirt with a cowhide vest over it, a man slung with a heavy pistol, a man as old as her father, his clothing unclean and in places raggy, and he stank of old sweat and whiskey and had foul breath.

"*Let me go!*" But she knew that saying it was futile.

"So you're Charlie Troy's juicy li'l whelp," Voller said. His grip on her was strong, and one-handed he was propelling her backwards, further in among the green brush. She was pulling and twisting but it was useless. "Wa'al, I got a message fer yer pa, an' it's this. If he ain't gone from here right soon, then there's men here that'll see to it that he does go, one way or another. We been around Cavan's already, an' we'll sure come ag'in." Chillingly, Imogen now knew for certain that there had been menace in the sounds of horses riding close by in the early morning. With a swift motion Voller let go her arm but just as quickly seized her hair where it was secured at the nape of her neck, and while she twisted this way and that, desperately trying to free herself, it was with revulsion that she felt his other hand moving over her body, over the thin fabric of her old dress, over her young breasts, down across her flat stomach, under it, between her legs. "An' then," Voller said, his breath foul in her face, "yuh won't have anybody, so we'll make yuh jump then, missy, by God we will."

Violently he flung her down in wet grass and as she lay gasping and sobbing, sore and humiliated, she heard him go swishing away and caught the sound of his low laughter.

6

ROB PURNELL was slammed backwards against a stack of empty crates, but although shocked, came away fast, hurting but now very angry.

They had been weaving and lurching and lashing out all round the yard, Rob Purnell, Dave Schiller and the red-headed Eddie Brady, hot breath vapouring in the chilly air.

Rob knew he was more than likely in some trouble, for whatever hesitations Schiller might have had yesterday, they were not evident now, and his belligerence had lent confidence to Brady. But they had left Rob with no option and must have known it, planned it, bustling Imogen along between them, spitting obscenities at her; and now as the three boys fought, striking out with red, raw knuckles, this time the girl had not taken the opportunity to run, but was pressed back against a wet board fence, clasping herself tightly under the dark blue cloak that Mary Purnell had brought her, the hood now hanging at her neck, her dark eyes wide and her heart pounding.

They were doing their utmost to work him into a bad situation where one would be in front of him, the other behind, but the Purnell boy was lithe and fast on his feet and proving difficult to trap. None the less he had taken a hard rap on the nose and bright blood was on his upper lip and chin.

Around they went, this way, that way, boots often slipping on the greasy hard-pack. Rob whipped in a swift punch at the bobbing Schiller and had the satisfaction — and felt the pain — of catching him on the left cheekbone, snapping the wall-eyed boy's head back.

Then Rob heard Imogen call out and when he was backing away from Schiller, was attacked from the side by Brady. Rob ducked his head but stood his ground, then hooked his right elbow back the way he had once seen a brawling cowboy do, and felt it bury itself in yielding flesh, and heard Brady scream, and when Rob went shuffling further back across the yard's slick surface, he saw the red-headed boy down on his knees, fingers pressed firmly to one eye, a high wailing sound now coming from him.

Yet here was Dave Schiller again, lumbering in, his breath coming hoarsely now and vapouring strongly, like some hard-worked beast, his skewed, enraged eyes aflame with malice. The power of his onslaught was sufficient to drive Rob Purnell backwards, but it had also made Schiller careless, over-confident of his strength, while Rob, calmer, now set his body compactly and drove his left fist through solidly against flesh and bone, the impact jolting him; but it stopped the bigger boy in his tracks, knocking his head back and in that bewildered instant Rob followed up, hooking his right fist in, the sound of it connecting with the side of Schiller's face a loud slap in the damp yard.

Dave Schiller went down like a shot dog, hurt and bleeding, while Rob Purnell stood over him, his chest heaving, his breath rasping, knuckles aflame with pain, the blood from his own nose now all down the front of his shirt.

Shaking his head like some street mutt, ignoring the keening, still-crouching, red-headed boy, Brady, Rob turned away, surprised then to find that, even though he had been conscious of her call, Imogen was still there, her back against the tall boards.

Out of slightly puffed lips, Rob said, "Come on."

Out on Main at a light-rippling, brimming trough the boy bent over and scooping his hands in, sluiced his head and face, the cold water sharpening his senses, stabbing fiercely at his hurts.

They walked together to the end of the street, the girl pale and silent, still shaken, he supposed, yet when he asked her if she was all right, she nodded. "Yes."

There was something more though, for her large, dark eyes were restless, looking down the way she must go to get to the Cavan place, from whose chimney blue woodsmoke was rising thinly.

"What's the matter, Imogen?"

It was then in uncertain words that rushed and stemmed by turns that she began to unburden herself of all there was to tell about the leather-legginged, stinking, raggy man who had stepped from the brush and grabbed hold of her, treated her roughly, threatened her and then fondled her.

The boy was startled, even momentarily uncomfortable, but he asked, "You tell your pa?" She nodded but only after a hesitation. There was still something wrong. "All of it?"

After another short pause she shook her head, looking away, colour now coming into her pale cheeks.

"No. Not all. Just that there'd been a man and what he looked like, and just about the . . . the threats he made about me and pa." The boy seemed to understand and did not press questions, and in any event she at once answered those he had left unspoken. "Pa's always told me to hold nothing back, what people might do, or say, that affects us. But I couldn't . . . I couldn't tell him everything about that, Rob. He's too ill. He would have got in a fine dander though. He would have tried to go out and find that man. My pa's too sick for that."

Hesitantly the boy reached out and touched one of her skinny shoulders and she did not instinctively pull away. It seemed to make more substantial a bond which had formed between them. Then in unspoken agreement he walked with her silently along the trail out of the town proper, just far enough so he could stand and watch her go hurrying to the derelict house and vanish around back of it. Rob turned away; but he had said to her, "Tomorrow, before school, I'll come fetch you."

★ ★ ★

In a rank alley in another part of Gabriel the steam was still rising from Voller's piss long after he had gone back inside to find that they had all tired of cards and that a couple of whores from upstairs, gaudy off-the-shoulder dresses inadequate for the cold conditions, had arrived looking for business.

Cam Hackman, seated at a table that was still littered with creased and finger-marked cards, his legs splayed out beneath it, with his long, horse face, his lantern jaw and his pale, resentful eyes that told of bigger defeats than the recent gambling had delivered him, looked up when Voller came pushing back towards him.

Under the hang of tobacco-smoke Voller resumed his seat. Hackman, in his old range clothing, was a dirty-skinned man, unshaven, the best-kept thing about him a scabbarded Remington .44 pistol with a cedar-handle and worn high on the left side, butt foremost. Hackman was inclined to fancy himself with it.

By now there must have been nearly two dozen people in this inadequate, bare-floored room among the scattering of chairs and two round tables, lamps hanging from hooks in the stained ceiling, a place whose atmosphere was ripe with sweat and cheap perfume; and Hackman, in this noisy gathering, was now quite restive. Paid off by Walsh out at the Tall W when he had counted on being kept on as a member of the winter crew, Hackman was fit to spit shit, and Voller thought it would not be very long before some unlucky bastard was made to pay for it. That had generally been Hackman's way, to seek out someone who was clearly vulnerable and exact a kind of revenge for his personal inadequacies.

Voller now chose to take advantage of that mood, since these doves did not appeal even to the likes of Hackman, and as far as Voller himself was concerned, he had acquired vastly different ambitions in that direction, ones that he was not about to share, and certainly not with Hackman. First, however, there was the matter of seeking a means to an end. So now, leaning a little closer to the rat-eyed, disgruntled cowman, Voller said, "I reckon it's high time this feller Troy was made to understand certain things."

* * *

Purnell, big, slightly stooped, his eyes hard, was doing his utmost to harness his anger.

Sent a message, invited to call at the mercantile, he had been somewhat taken aback to discover nearly a dozen and a half townsmen already in there, all come for the same purpose. Now for the first time he thought he could see the extent of feeling that had been whipped up, probably across counters, at saloon tables, on street corners, over the presence of Charlie Troy.

A dim-cornered place even on the brightest of days, it was today a cavern of shadows among the assorted merchandise, in spite of several lamps having been lit. All present were standing, all wearing heavy coats or slickers and smelling of dampness and the prevailing sour odours of the town. In some places, after rain, the very essence of the good earth rises up to excite the senses. In places such as Gabriel, however, whenever rain ceased, the odours borne upon the heavy air were more often representative of cold mud, dung and putrefying garbage.

George Crimond, though he was Gabriel's leading citizen, standing there in his derby hat and wearing an ulster, did not immediately speak up, nor did others, some of whom were recognizable as members of the town council. Not too surprisingly, in Purnell's view, Hawtrey, who was not, was the one to lead off.

"I'll not beat about the bush, Purnell," Hawtrey said, looking down his bold beak, "there's been a lot of talk and a lot of concern raised about this man Troy. Now, people have come here to this town over a hell of a long time, some of 'em have stayed, some not. That's the way of it, all over. But this man we're talking about, he's different. We all know it. If he stays here we reckon it's only a matter of time before he attracts some of the real scum to Gabriel. Men will come looking for him. It's happened in other places, so we've heard. It's said he draws 'em wherever he goes. We don't want that here. We don't intend to have it happen."

"I know, Henry," Purnell said as easily as he could, "I've heard all that same talk. I've heard some people say that Charlie's like to fetch a kind of plague behind him, all that."

Now blinking his closely-set, button eyes, George Crimond said, "It's true. What's been said is all true. There's been talk brought in from all over." He began floundering, then said, "We've got enough problems around here without him."

For a moment or two Purnell looked up at one of the ancient, smoky lamps as though suddenly conscious of the thick, fetid atmosphere, the shifting of too many feet and the overpowering proximity of damp clothing. He bided his time, then returned to the line he had taken at the beginning, when they had first approached him.

"He's in very poor shape, is Troy, much too bad to travel on in that wagon; an' not only that, he's got this young girl to think of. But he doesn't plan on staying around Gabriel an hour longer than he has to. I've talked with him. That's what he says an' that's what I believe."

One of the councillors, a seedy little man named Meares, his coat powdered with cigar-ash and who had always given an impression that he was somewhat overawed when in Purnell's presence, now spoke up unexpectedly, saying in his whispery fashion, "It's not that we want to, ah, be in any way, ah, unfair, Mr Purnell, especially not towards the, ah, child. Word is sure getting around though. Folks on the stages, travelling through, they're starting to, ah, ask questions about, ah, Troy. Soon, well we, ah, don't know, do we . . . ?" As though all at once aware of his own voice he glanced around anxiously, perhaps seeking evidence of approval for speaking at all and when none was immediately evident, subsided and said no more.

As though Meares had not spoken, Hawtrey said, "Purnell, I hear what it is you're saying. We all do. But the hours an' the days are going by an' this man is still around, an' we've only got" — blinking and balking at last — "only got *his* word on how sick he really is."

"Vern Likens," said Purnell tightly. "By now you'll all have heard Vern's opinion."

"Well, yeah. Yeah. But Vern, y'know, he's the nearest we got to a regular doc, an' they, well, sometimes they take a kinda *soft* view." Hawtrey moved his shoulders as though suddenly chilled and now did not seem to want to look directly at Purnell. "If this Troy — " He stopped, then started again. "If this Troy should get too . . . comfortable here, get a few folks' sympathy, get too much done for him, that sort of thing, he might be inclined to hang around a lot longer." They had indeed put a halter on their own women, Purnell thought, that much had become clear, but this would be as close as they would get to admitting it.

Purnell knew too that what had been said was intended as a personal rebuke and was aimed at Mary as much as himself, perhaps even at young Rob, and he gave Hawtrey a long, direct stare sufficient to compel the merchant once again to avoid meeting his eyes.

"When we stop offering help where it's plainly needed," he said, "when even the women stop short of it, we might as well go the whole hog and start shooting any pilgrims that happen to turn up sick."

A flush rose in Hawtrey's long face but he refused to respond to words which must have struck at him, and he said, "I do hear that his child's been comin' up to the school."

"She has."

"That seems to say to me they're here for some while."

"They're here for as long as it takes," said Purnell doggedly, "an' I've given Charlie Troy to understand he's not about to be evicted."

During this discussion Purnell had noticed that Abe Kettley had come in and now saw him easing through the group of men, his eastern-style hat in his hand, the bilious lamplight shining off his pale ivory baldness.

"I sure do hope," Kettley said, "If

there's any trouble blows up over Troy being here in this community, that you're ready to stand by that decision, Brad, one that you made, not the town council."

"I am," said Purnell. He now believed that if he were to stay in this place for much longer, the way things seemed to be headed, he might well get into a rough argument that could lead to something a lot worse, and he felt he owed Mary and his son more than that. He nodded to them and walked out of the mercantile, hearing an urgent murmuring of voices gathering at his back.

★ ★ ★

They had gone down there afoot, moving between dripping branches, both wearing high-collared, studded leather jackets, both belching and trailing fumes of raw spirit, and though the distance was not great, it was far enough, going by the circuitous route they had thought prudent, and in the wet conditions, to start Hackman complaining long before they got there; so much so that in the finish Voller, coming to the last clumps of brush that screened them from the Cavan place, said, "Keep it down, Hack, or the bastard'll hear yuh comin'."

Hackman, still sniffing and grumbling, but in a marginally lowered voice, was swatting droplets from his ill-used hat. It was very late in the day now, dusk, and what with the leaden overcast and all, visibility was much reduced. They had arrived at a spot that lay behind Cavan's, just short of the grassy, weed-infested yard, squinting between a couple of dilapidated outbuildings at the sorry-looking house itself.

Hackman suddenly said, "Light. There."

Voller moved a step closer, leaning forward, peering. It was so, as he could see. Though a ragged curtain had been pulled across one of the back windows, a yellowish light was indeed glimmering there.

Presently Voller muttered, "Sick or no, the bastard's still Charlie Troy. It's best we git some distance between us so we kin git a shot two ways. We got to nail him real quick. No chances."

Head still buzzing with the effects of liquor or not, Hackman could understand that, yet he gave an odd-sounding chuckle, clearly warming to the notion, now that they had actually come this far, of being remembered forever as the man who took the great Charlie Troy. Hackman had not commented at any stage on the fact that there would be a young girl inside the house as well, perhaps because he had forgotten all about her.

But Voller certainly had not.

* * *

Near to the death of the day a brooding heaviness of heart had overtaken Purnell, for he had come home from the unsatisfactory meeting at the mercantile to listen in silence as Mary related all that the boy had told her, of the bruising fight in the yard (for Rob had had to give an explanation for the state he had been in) but mostly what had happened to Imogen Troy at the hands of a man in leather leggings.

"Voller," Purnell had said at once. "Dirty, stinking, a cowhide vest, leather leggings with metal studs. Voller."

Mary was now deeply concerned for the safety of the child.

"He *touched* her, Brad, and she had to hold that back from her pa, for fear that, ill as he might be, he'd try to go out and find the man. Imogen shouldn't have to carry that kind of burden. No young girl should."

"She told Rob though."

"Yes, maybe because she had to tell *somebody*; somebody she thought she could trust. But, Rob, well, he's relieved that *I* know, now, but at the same time he was ashamed of repeating it, as though he'd given away a confidence."

"He's upstairs?"

"Yes."

"I'll talk with him. But for all we know, maybe the girl was hoping he might tell you." He drew a deep breath. "Voller. Never can be sure which way he'll jump."

"I was right about that man bringing trouble. Could he turn out to be really dangerous, or is he only a braggart?"

"With enough liquor in him he could turn real ugly, an' he's got a few friends that I'd as soon see right out of Gabriel." Purnell rubbed a broad hand over his face. "God damn Voller. There's already enough to keep an eye on." He told her what had transpired up at the mercantile. "They didn't push it as hard as they might do yet, but there were enough of them in that place to show me what it is building up. Hawtrey, he's the one at the centre of it. But all they need is one voice — one like Hawtrey's, loud enough, often enough." Wearily he walked across and picked up his hat and his jacket. "I'll go take a look around, see if I can locate Ed Voller, warn him off before it gets any worse."

"Brad, your supper's near to ready."

"I'll not be long." She did not attempt to dissuade him but he did pause in the doorway. "It's for the girl's sake, first. The other thing is, if Voller is hanging around near Cavan's already, he could go there again any time, an' Charlie's got no rifle, no pistol even. So if anything goes wrong he could be a dead man before his time."

7

THE half-light of dusk was now all but gone.

Voller and Hackman had separated, Hackman cutting wide, swishing through long, wet grass, passing behind the grey bulk of the barn, the sounds of his movements fading and finally ceasing, and such as it was, the plan was for Hackman eventually to make an approach from the opposite side of what had been the Cavan yard.

Voller, having followed first by eye and then by ear the shambling departure of Hackman, now, the Forehand and Wadsworth in his fist, and after a long squint at what little of the main building he could see from where he was, began to go edging around the half-collapsed outbuilding at his elbow.

Once he had picked his way to

the farther corner, the overgrown yard itself spread before him. Some twenty yards from his right shoulder stood the barn, and if he had not been conscious of them earlier, he was now aware of the snuffling and shifting of horses inside; Troy's wagon-team, no doubt. And there, outside the barn, the wagon itself, no trooped canvas on it at this time, a sturdy vehicle with casks secured to its sides and a long storage-box like that to be seen on chuck-wagons, at the rear. In the weedy grasses there were a couple of partly-recovered swathes marking where it had been drawn to the place where it now stood.

Voller moved on, the chill catching at him now, in his nostrils the sharp tang of woodsmoke from the chimney, the warming effects of the liquor he had drunk now beginning to wear off. Across the front of the darkly-shadowed outbuilding he went, then across the narrow gap between it and the next, a less damaged structure this, one with a slight roof-overhang. Deep in shadow Voller's eyes fastened now on the slivers of light at the only visible window. Voller paused, casting a look in the direction from which he expected Hackman to appear, to make some sign of readiness, no simple matter, perhaps, in this early evening gloom.

Voller froze, his head turning slowly. A door-latch had clicked. In near disbelief, gripping the Forehand and Wadsworth, he saw light and shadows altering and then the figure of the child was standing on the porch framed in the dull glow from the yard door. Voller could hear his own breathing harsh in his throat, and his half-raised pistol began drifting down.

Then something else, a whisper of movement in the dark behind him and an unyielding object pressing into his lower back, and the short-breathed, husky-voice of the bone-man warmed his left ear.

"Too bad, mister."

Sweat that had gone suddenly cold

formed between Voller's shoulder-blades and when the pressure in his back eased a reaching hand took hold of his pistol and now he was breathing shortly with shock, and in a sense naked; and sober.

Out of an eerie stillness the cocking of the Forehand and Wadsworth seemed inordinately loud. From a clothes-rustling sound Voller got the impression that signs were being made, signs perhaps just visible to the child still watching from the porch, for the next moment she had gone and in moments after that, the light inside the house, poor as it had been, died altogether.

Where in the name of Christ was Hack?

Hackman was coming, albeit tardily. After all a man had to piss.

Was that him now, a shapeless shadow across the wilderness of weeds and giving out faint sounds?

Voller then emitted a low moan and bent his head and pressed a hand to his stomach, whispering *"Jesus!"* and he had the impression that the man behind him had eased further away, puzzled perhaps by Voller's evident distress.

Voller sank down, then went sprawling in the weeds and no sooner had he done so, knowing that Hackman could not have failed to hear, screamed, "*Now! Nail the bastard!*"

The gunflash was bright and immediate, and nearby timber took a whacking impact, but when Voller screwed his face around for a glimpse, it was to see the indistinct shape of a man down on one knee, an impression of a raised, crooked elbow, the pistol laid across it for relief of weight as much as steadincss, Voller's own .44, which then erupted with a flashing explosion that made Voller's ears ring, and he actually heard the lead hit Hackman and then heard Hackman's scream amid thrashing sounds among the weeds and long grass across the yard.

Not knowing of the agony, the waves of sweating nausea now overtaking the shooter behind him, for a moment Voller remained where he was, then came slowly to his feet. The smell of spent powder hung richly on the cold air. Out in what was now darkness Hackman was continuing to make outrageous noises.

The yard-door latch again. Something pale across there. The girl. Troy's voice, though not strong, carried to her.

"Immy, go fetch the marshal."

Hearing the man speak again, the strained, short-breathed nature of the words offered Voller some hope, but he dare not move too soon. The noises coming from Hackman were diminishing, his energy draining away with his life essences. *What a shit of a way and a shit of a place to die.*

Voller forced himself into a kind of calm, the child long gone running, melting into farther darkness, clothes, pale flesh winking, leaving a silence except for the bubbly breathing of Charlie Troy behind him, half dead but deadly, all the killings of Troy's past crouching at Voller's back.

But the corner of this outbuilding was a mere foot to Voller's left-hand side, and he waited, hang-headed, hoping that the reason that there were no further words was that Troy no longer had the strength to form them. But Voller could *not* see him; and Troy was armed. Yet Voller had no intention of waiting like some goddamn' sheep for the marshal to come. He could expect no mercy from Purnell.

Voller was gone before Troy could even raise the pistol for the weapon had acquired extraordinary weight and was now hanging at his side, the broken pump-handle with which he had first bluffed Voller long ago laid aside. Troy leaned against a none-too-solid wall, his light frame unlikely to make undue demands on it.

After a minute or so Troy resolved to attempt to get back to the house. Whether or not the man he had brought down was still alive he did not know and he did not have the desire — or the strength — to go fumbling around in the dark in order to find out. That was unfortunate as he was soon to discover, but for the moment he gave his full attention to getting himself from where he was now, across to the back porch.

An almost unnatural quiet had fallen after the sudden fierce riot of gunfire. Like a man walking a high wire Troy went step by careful step through the knee-high growth, making only small chesty sounds until, his head and face and neck slick with sweat, he gained the porch and laboriously made his way up onto it, stumbling slightly at the last.

That was the particular sound that pin-pointed him, that Voller, having circled and come around by Hackman's route and arrived at Hackman's dead and stinking body, now plainly heard even as, feeling around in wet grass, his hand closed over Hack's fallen Remington pistol.

Trembling from his efforts, breathing huskily, Troy all but voided his bladder from shock when Voller shot flickeringly at him and lead came slamming into the woodwork of the porch. Yet even in his reduced and pitiful state, the reflexes of time, born of wild gunfire in rat-holes of places now all but forgotten, up against men ten times the measure of Voller, still responded. Troy was on his bony knees, pistol laid across the porch rail and blasting once, twice in gunflare and acrid fumes at the vaguest of vague shapes some fifty feet away from him. He did not hit the man but fanned him with a lethal breath, and that was it for Voller who turned and went charging into deeper darkness, perhaps imagining he could hear, too, the approach of others, while Troy, near senseless from shock and from his exertions, lay slumped against the porch railing, gripping the cedar butt of the Forehand and Wadsworth as though it were some staunch handle of salvation, preventing him from sliding backwards into the horrors of the Pit.

That was how Purnell and Likens, arriving in the druggist's two-horse buggy, found him and helped him inside.

By the time Mary arrived, afoot, having persuaded Imogen to stay with Rob near the warmth of the stove in the Purnell house, Purnell himself had become satisfied that Voller had indeed left the immediate area and that the cowboy, Hackman, was dead.

"Got a-hold of Hackman's pistol, right enough," Purnell said, "an' his shell-belt."

It would be later, in Gabriel, that word would be passed that Voller had been seen, mounted up and heading out, north-eastward.

Troy was now in some distress, for that evening he had made a supreme effort and though Likens did what he could, Troy was limp, seeming almost lifeless. Mary, pulling up the hood of her cloak, leaving to go back with Likens in his buggy, had prepared food for the following day, gathered up Imogen's nightdress together with some clothing to be laundered. For the remainder of this night, she had said, Imogen would be given a bed at the Purnell house so that Troy himself might rest, his mind free, knowing that the child was in safe hands.

Purnell said he would sit here for a while, for the Gabriel undertaker, Edlin, would have to be rousted out, presumably by Likens, and whether Edlin wished to or not, come out to remove the body of the dead cowboy, Hackman.

Purnell first fetched in more wood and dumped it into a box near the stove, then waved a hand towards the coffee-pot, raising his eyebrows. Troy, yellow, resting back in the old hide-covered chair, boots splayed out before him, thought about it, then nodded, lids drooping, but he said, "Might be a wise move to supply a bowl as well, marshal." Sometimes his food or drink was soon vomited.

"Well," said Purnell eventually, coffee-mug in hand, "now there's two more of 'em that knows better."

Troy's thin mouth formed into the bleakest of smiles and when he could summon sufficient breath, he said, "What I was doing I was doing from memory." Then, "I'm beholden to your wife, Brad, for what she's done, an' your boy for what he's done, looking out for Immy."

With a slight movement of a hand Purnell dismissed any notion of obligation. He did not have the heart to tell the man the whole of it, about Voller and Imogen. Still, with any sort of luck they might have seen the last of Voller. With any sort of luck. Sourly, Purnell thought that it was folly for a man to put any trust in luck. As though he might have been reading the mind of the other man, Troy, though slurring his words slightly, for Likens' medication was beginning to take hold, said, "The fat we talked about, it's in the fire now, no mistake. This'll be what they've been waiting for." He meant, of course, the townsmen of Gabriel.

Purnell sipped his coffee, saying nothing, for there was little he could have said; and in Charlie Troy's voice there had been a distinct sense that he saw that his time had run out in this place too.

★ ★ ★

For Purnell it had moved on some way from the shifty-eyed, uneasy congress of the mercantile. As even Troy himself had predicted, there was a firming of attitude — for most of those same men were present — word having spread more quickly in the damply unpleasant hours than even Purnell would have thought probable.

They were not in the mercantile this time, however, they were inside or standing around near the premises of Edlin, the Gabriel undertaker, a sour man with a ragged yellow moustache, bad teeth and infinitely worse breath.

As Purnell had surmised, Edlin had not relished having to go up to Cavan's with his glass-sided hearse on such a cold night, with further rain threatening at any moment, to the stench-laden aftermath of gunfire that had been clearly heard in the town proper.

It did seem that there had been an instinctive realization of what the shooting had meant, shooting from that particular direction. *Charlie Troy.*

A surprising number of people, those who did not mind the room-enclosed amalgamated smells of human sweat and faeces, lye soap and formaldehyde and blood, had been inside Edlin's to view the remains of the once-cowboy, Cam Hackman, gut-shot, probably by a slug which had been gouged to distort on impact, his intestines rudely protruding.

Purnell, for his part, having also observed the cadaver, deeply regretted that Troy had failed in his attempt to kill Ed Voller.

If Henry Hawtrey's had been the

predominant voice at the mercantile, Kettley's was being heard most clearly, at least for a start, at Edlin's.

"Well," Kettley said from under his fine eastern hat, standing on the boardwalk in his ulster just outside Edlin's frontage, and allowing his words to include the maybe twenty huddled, assorted townsmen there, while looking at Purnell who had just emerged, "so this is what it's now coming to."

If Purnell had considered saying anything in response to that he was forestalled by Hawtrey, followed by Crimond, squeezing out from the doorway, Crimond's face the colour and apparent consistency of baker's dough, his button eyes sunk in it like currants.

"Indeed," Hawtrey said, "it *is* what it's come to, an' it's *exactly*, marshal, *exactly* what we wanted you to hear and to heed when we were over at the mercantile. That dead man in there is there because of this man Troy, put there by Troy's own hand." Hawtrey's voice had been rising as he spoke and at the end he was breathing hard and his eyes were tending to protrude.

From his new-found position of political strength, Kettley said, "This simply can't be allowed to go on. I've heard there were two men up there. The other lit out, but what guarantee is there that he won't soon be back, or that others like him won't come, and there'll be more shooting and more killing?"

Purnell said harshly, "If those two bastards hadn't gone near Cavan's, if Hackman hadn't shot at Troy, he wouldn't be lying in there now with shit coming out his belly."

Kettley licked dry lips, breath clouding whitely in the cold air. "We've only got Troy's word on what happened — or you have."

"Hackman was shot with Voller's pistol. Sick as he is, Charlie Troy took it from Voller and had to use it because he didn't have one of his own."

There was a short silence, only clouded breathing in flung lamplight, eyes blinking under brims of hats, a hunching under jackets and coats. Oddly, it was Crimond who said, plucking the same string as had Kettley, "We've got to do something about this. We've got no choice." The voices muttering in support of that were mainly those of the several town councillors present.

Purnell could see and hear and sense that this was a vastly different meeting — for a kind of public meeting it was, though this group had simply coagulated here rather than having been specially called — than the one at the mercantile. None the less he came back unswervingly to what he had already told a number of these same men.

"Charlie Troy's in bad shape. I've told him he can stay where he is for a long as it takes to get his strength back before he moves on." And he repeated, "What went on up there tonight wasn't of Troy's making."

Before he had even finished saying it, Hawtrey's head was shaking and so was Crimond's.

"That's just not good enough, Purnell." This was Crimond again, unusually assertive as though he had made up his mind about it long before this or maybe, mayor or not, had had it made up for him. "We've come to a decision that the time for talk is done with now. Everybody's real edgy, the womenfolk in particular."

Purnell's hard eyes bored into the plump, whey-faced man, Mary's words still in Purnell's ear concerning Phena Crimond's generously-powdered face. " . . . *some of it was there to try to cover a bruise on her cheekbone . . .* "

"So your mind an' the council's mind," Purnell said, "is that Troy goes, regardless of what I've told him as the marshal here?"

"That's it," Crimond said, if slightly less confidently. "That's what we've decided."

"So you, Purnell, as the town

marshal," Kettley put in, "whatever it is you happen to have told this man, you're the one who's got to get on up there and tell him different."

"He's broken no law, no town ordinance," Purnell said. "What Troy did he did in his own defence."

"They were there only because *he* was there," Kettley persisted, "which was what we all said would happen sooner or later. You don't want the vermin, you get rid of the bait."

"That puts it neat," said Hawtrey, "tied up an' tidy."

A firm murmur of agreement came on the heels of that and Purnell had to admit, if only to himself, that from their point of view it made every kind of sense. Fear was a powerful goad and without doubt these men were now going in fear; you could almost smell it hanging in the cold air. But it was the careless lack of compassion attending their self-interest that thrust at him. He thought then of Mary and of young Rob, both of whom were completely dependent on *him*, but he knew as only he *could* know that no matter what he decided, Mary would stand by him. It was, he reflected, a certainty enjoyed by perhaps few of the men now staring at him out on this bleak street.

"I've done whatever I could," he said then, "about the vermin that have come here to Gabriel from time to time, an' I carry some scars because of it. I'd do it again, come the need. But I'll not move against Charlie Troy. He'll not be run out of Gabriel by me, an' if by your lights that's a breach, then so be it."

Kettley again licked at his lips, blinking, as though he thought he might not have heard it right. Crimond, also blinking his little eyes, after some seconds of almost complete silence, said, "Let me get this straight, Mr Purnell, are you saying to us that if he goes, you go? I mean, that you'd no longer serve as marshal?"

Purnell had not said that directly but what he *had* said probably amounted to the same thing; but Crimond had put it up front, baldly, so there could be no possible misunderstanding.

"Well then," said Kettley for the want of something better.

"Can't get any plainer than that," said Hawtrey.

If there were some among them who doubted the wisdom of what now seemed inexorably to be on the move here — and Purnell thought he did detect some genuine hesitations — Crimond then put it beyond all doubt by saying, "Then you don't leave us an option, Mr Purnell."

Twenty minutes later, Purnell, stepping inside his own warm kitchen, did not have to explain to Mary, looking up from her chair, that there was trouble. Even if the missing badge of office had not done it, then Purnell's expression would have. When he had told her, she repeated the one name.

"Kettley."

"Yeah. Acting town marshal until such time as elections can be held."

"They've wanted this all along, that faction," she said. There was bitter resentment in the way she said it but no fear for herself or for their son.

"We'll have to talk about what we should do," he said. For a moment he wondered if he really did have the right to alter all their lives in this way, just like that, on some point of principle that involved a man who was already dying and to whom he owed nothing.

"Whatever we do," she said, "we'll be together, you, me and Rob. As for talking, we'll leave that 'til tomorrow. And I want to go up to Cavan's again. If you won't abandon them, neither will I."

Purnell touched her shoulders, then gathered her to him, his large hands rubbing up and down her firm, narrow back.

8

FOLLOWING even short periods of activity Charlie Troy was now compelled to sit down for a time to recover. He was doing this now, breathing deeply; but his eyes were bright today and he had been most attentive to all Purnell had been saying. Mary, who had been working around the house, and Likens who had been checking on Troy, had now departed. Imogen had been called for by Rob, leaving Troy and Purnell together.

It was clear that Troy had been much concerned by what he had heard and he came back now to something he had started to say earlier.

"Not worth it, Brad. Soon I'll be run out of here anyway, or I'll be dead. You'll still be here, your wife an' your boy to take care of, an' now you've got no work. Is the house yours?"

"No," Purnell said, "it belongs to the town, comes with the marshal's job; but Abe Kettley's got his own place, so he won't need it. I can't see 'em pushing that issue, not yet awhile, anyway." Indeed, this was a matter which, so far, had not been mentioned by Crimond or anybody else and one which Purnell himself had not yet sought to discuss with Mary. But the question of the house was not his immediate concern. "As far as the marshal's job goes, it was in the balance anyway. It's an office that comes by election. This man Kettley, Mayor Crimond's brother-in-law, he'd already thrown his hat in the ring. There's been some moves afoot for a while behind closed doors, to make a change. Just simmering. But I've got to say that this Kettley was a surprise. I've got doubts that he'd have enough sand to make a hard point stick if he had to."

"Political." It was said slowly and quietly. Purnell thought that Troy was probably recalling personal experience. "No doubt of that."

Troy nodded, endured a spasm of violent coughing, then sat pressing spidery fingers to his sternum, thereafter breathing in a laboured and wheezy manner. Eventually: "Your boy got in some trouble, so I hear, on account of Immy. I knew he was watching out for her. I'm real sorry he got hurt."

"Yeah. Well it's over an' done with now. Come an' gone, so Rob tells me."

Troy's deeply sunken eyes tracked Purnell soberly as he went pacing up the long room and back again. Then: "The horses in good shape?"

Purnell nodded. "Plenty of feed, plenty of water." Purnell had seen to that, for Troy, today, had had to turn back, trying to get as far as the barn. Purnell knew, however, that behind the question lay an assumption on Troy's part that he would soon be compelled to try to harness the team to the wagon once again. Now that Purnell, whose office and whose attitude had afforded him some protection was no longer in a position to do so, it must only be a question of time before the harsh ultimatum would be delivered; but he asked:

"Any word of Voller?"

"No," said Purnell, "*Seen leaving* means no more than that. Keep your eyes peeled if you can, would be my advice." he had left with Troy a box of .44 ammunition. At the door he paused, glanced back at the sad, shrunken man sitting in the chair. "I'll be back, Charlie."

Troy raised one of his skeletal hands, let it drop again. Purnell left.

Mary Purnell, leaving Main on her way home with a laden basket, nodded civilly but tight-lipped to Abe Kettley, Acting-Marshal. Kettley, who in passing, had raised his conservative hat to her. The obsequious smile, the brief flash of his bald head, the neat fussiness of his appearance caused her to view the badge pinned ostentatiously to his coat as patently absurd. "*He'll never be up to it,*" she thought, yet that did not alter the fact that he was there, and his permanent appointment must be reasonably certain. Her mood at the present time was not good. On her domestic expedition in and out of some Gabriel shops she had encountered several other townswomen, but all of them, although courteous enough, were *much too occupied just at this moment* to stop and talk with her about the Troys. The further Mary went that morning the more irritated she became. Seeing Abe Kettley flaunting the badge that for so long had been worn by her husband had certainly done nothing to improve her day.

The affair of the Gabriel marshal was of course being talked about elsewhere in the town. One man had a particular interest. In what once had been the office of a lumber yard, a company that in hard times had folded long ago, and sited on a back street, a structure dripping after recent rain, three men were sprawled, sheltering, talking laconically. The yard outside was a place almost ringed by outbuildings and poled shelters grey with age and with weathering, of grass and of black-wet baulks of abandoned lumber.

The bottle was holding out, going the rounds again. There was an unwashed, whiskered cowman from Walsh's Tall W, come into town to collect some supplies, his wagon and team standing in the sea of grass, the second a ruddy-complexioned man in black pants, brown, food-stained vest and striped blue shirt, a dented derby on his head, this one an out-of-work bartender. And Ed Voller.

Voller's horse, long-hitched to one of the lengths of lumber, the bit slipped, was cropping lush grass.

The cowman was named Eadie, the ex-bartender Ames, and both of them had been long-time drinking companions of the man in the studded leggings.

"So," Voller said. "Purnell's gone, by God. Now there's a piece o' luck."

"Well, he ain't *gone*, it's jes' he ain't the marshal no more," said Ames, wiping his mouth with a grubby shirt-sleeve. Eadie received the bottle, took a gulping swig, hissed breath out after it, coughed, handed the bottle to Voller.

After a moment Eadie said, "I don't reckon much to this Kettley, apart from shootin' any stray dawgs on Main."

Ames belched deeply and with evident satisfaction. "Reckon he's got the sand to move Charlie Troy on?"

Voller drank deeply, the fiery spirit making his eyes water, but its warmth was now coursing through him, easing out of him the stiffness of his cold night-camp; but what Ames had just said was also burning him because what he had come to see as his humiliation at Troy's hands — at the hands of a man already walking towards death — had invaded his mind, eating at him, goading him to a point at which he seemed to see erstwhile companions

148

looking sideways at him, even smiling. *"It was Ed that lit out with his ass afire when it was Charlie Troy who farted."*

Voller blinked grainy eyes at the images of Ames and Eadie which had now joined into one, then disengaged, but one and then the other trembled in his vision. Voller thought about Abe Kettley too, at this time, and toyed with a drink-inflamed notion of openly approaching him, but discarded that, at least for the present. Voller took another gasping swig, then passing the bottle to Ames who, earlier, had fetched some grub back for Voller and who now asked:

"What now, then, Ed? Where to now? Back to the spread?"

Voller scraped black fingernails through his itching whiskers and shrugged. The spread. The hell with the spread. It had about gone belly-up, anyway. "Right now I'm gonna throw the bedroll down in here, git some more shut-eye." He was probing around in a pocket of his pants and presently brought out several crumpled bills, one of which he handed to Ames. "I could use another bottle an' some more grub."

Ames nodded, thrust the bill into a pocket. Eadie, who had been sitting on the floor propped against a wall, stood up slowly, his joints cracking. "Got to git goin' boys."

"Remember," Voller said, glancing from one to the other, "keep your goddamn' teeth shut over this."

Once they were gone he would have time to think it over, sit finishing the bottle. Suddenly the image of Troy's girl came swimming into his mind and he watched Ames and Eadie leave and raised the bottle to his mouth.

It had begun raining again, but lightly.

Mary Purnell was still feeling upset, her cheeks faintly flushed.

"You can't flat-out accuse them," Purnell said, but only in an attempt to appease her.

Mary, however, was in no fit humour to be comforted. "Brad, I know quite well when I'm being put off deliberately. I think I'd even accept it if just one of them would have the nerve — no, the decency — to stand right in front of me and tell me the truth, that they do sympathize with the Troys, with the fix those folks are in, but their men have had the last word. *Stay well clear of the Troys. And stay clear of the Purnell woman because she's getting involved with them.* That's all I'd ask of them Brad, honesty. I thought I knew them well enough for that. I was wrong, and it hurts."

"I know," said Purnell, "an' I'm real sorry that you've got hurt. But what you an' I have to do now is talk about us, whether we're going to stay here in Gabriel, try to get other work — "

"Some hope of that, Brad, the way things are."

" — or whether we ought to up stakes an' move on, an' if we do, to where? For a start we could try

151

Shearman. Or I could go there an' if I managed to find work, send for you an' Rob." He had not sounded in the least alarmed, counting off what sounded like possibilities, when he knew, and Mary knew, that his chances of his finding work to keep them all, either in Shearman or anywhere else in the county at the present time, were minimal. Yet he persisted. "There's Wells Fargo. Could be possibilities there." Another kite going up, and Mary knew that, too.

She moved in behind his chair and placed her long hands flat against his chest and bent her face to his. "We'll manage, Brad. We'll come through it. We've done it before and we'll do it again." when he nodded, she said, "You'll still do what you can for the Troy's? *We* will?"

"Yeah. I'll not abandon Charlie now."

"Nor will I. I'm not about to join these people here. I don't bow to Crimond or Hawtrey or Kettley, no matter what, while I'm still here in Gabriel, and no matter what the other women think or do."

The day passed in a strange, restrained way under louring clouds, with intermittent light rain, and Abe Kettley had still made no move to go on up to the Cavan place to give Troy the hard word. Kettley, however, had been doing plenty of walking up and down Main, calling into this place and that, wearing the badge.

Now dusk had come down, the darker for the presence of the heavy overcast, and Voller, his face aflame with the liquor he had drunk, blinking eyes that were grainy, was once again within sight of Cavan's.

Pistol in hand and cocked, Voller came shuffling along the side of the great barn, hearing movements of the horses inside, and at the corner of the building he paused, peering through the gloom towards the faintly-lighted house. Then he moved on, skirting the Troy wagon, swishing through the rain-beaded grasses, solidly wet enough to tug at him as he went, pistol held before him, no precise plan in his mind, his thinking, in any event, clouded by liquor.

So Voller was only a matter of fifty feet away from the back porch when he realized that someone else was in the yard, and even as this perception came to him, whoever it was — a man — called, "Who's that?"

Voller shot immediately in a bright flicker and a blast of noise and by the yell and the welter of confused movement that followed knew that he had got a hit, and the target seemed to have gone down fast.

What happened next was almost too quick for Voller to apprehend for seemingly all at the same instant what little light was showing inside the house went out, the yard door on the porch was wrenched open and a man's shape was coming out in one hell of a rush, a tall man by the looks, the dull gleam of a pistol in his hand. No shuffling invalid this, but someone big and energetic who without doubt had seen Voller, had probably witnessed his shooting from within and who now in turn let go a bright, blasting shot at Voller and hit him hard, the pistol in Voller's hand only partly raised.

Down into the wet, tangled grass Voller went, the handle of the Remington suddenly feeling like wet soap, so that it went sliding from his grasp. Once down, Voller tried to sit up but fell back, a warm richness welling up in him, filling his mouth and bringing a blood-smell along with the sharper tang of spent powder-fumes. When, his stomach convulsing, he emptied his mouth, what came gouting out was warm and sticky, and as small bright sparks came dancing across his vision, he discovered, too, that the night was receding into velvet silence.

Voller therefore did not hear clearly Purnell's hard voice because he was now almost beyond all hearing and all seeing, retching, vomiting more blood, dying in the wet grass.

Purnell had not in fact been talking to Voller but to the man Voller had shot, and now, under a lantern being borne slowly outside by Charlie Troy, he saw that the hurt man was Abe Kettley. "*Come to do the business in the dark*," Purnell thought, "*an' found Voller instead.*"

Then Purnell did move across to the fallen Voller. Dying, certainly, but in the final moments coming to a first and last realization of the man who was bending over him in the lantern's light, Voller was mumbling a jumble of words to urgent questioning; then dying. No coming back now, the bending man gone, and gone the last vestige of light.

Purnell straightened, took the lantern from Troy's thin, shaking hand. "Go back inside, Charlie."

Purnell himself returned to Kettley. Gabriel's acting marshal had taken lead high on his left side, lead that maybe had touched a rib — broken it, perhaps — cutting thin flesh there and passing on. Pained and bloodied Kettley was, moaning deeply, looking like a white slug, his fine hat flown away, his bald head gleaming.

To Troy, still going slowly in, Purnell, in an odd, harsh voice, said, "I'll go fetch Likens for this rooster. I'll hammer on Edlin's door as well while I'm there."

Troy made no answer but Purnell heard his muffled voice telling Imogen that it was over, to go back to her bed.

* * *

They were not murmuring now but all talking at once, in the cold morning, up at the mercantile, hats and coats dripping on the bare wood floor, Mabel Hawtrey there too, handing out mugs of steaming coffee but of course taking no part in the discussion, a pale, silent wraith coming and going.

Abe Kettley was absent, not without

reason, at home nursing his wound, treated and bound up by Vern Likens and assured somewhat brusquely that his life was in no way threatened.

And there was an unseen presence, at this time laid out in Edlin's odiferous parlour, but which, in absentia, had been at the very centre of this meeting. "*First Hackman, now Voller.*" And but for vagrant chance, they assumed, they might also have been discussing the death of Abe Kettley. Nobody seemed to want to mention the name Purnell, at least not at this stage.

Crimond had come late to this gathering, his round face looking pastier than ever, for he was fresh from the bedside of his brother-in-law and from under the tongue of his own sister, Crimond apparently now viewed as one of the architects of her husband's misfortune, the euphoric status of marshaldom swiftly forgotten.

"Merge has got herself into something of a state," Crimond reported, "and she swears by the Almighty that it's the finish of Abe standing for regular marshal."

Hawtrey favoured the Gabriel mayor with a somewhat thin-lipped look, then raised his own voice to quieten the gathering. Mabel Hawtrey shrank away into shadows.

"With all this that's happened up to now," Hawtrey said, "it's not going to get any better, it can only get worse. Troy's got to go, an' he's got to be told right soon. Purnell's taken his side but Purnell's got no authority."

Meares ventured the obvious. "There is no, ah, marshal at all, as such." He looked at George Crimond. "Do you, ah, plan on appointing another acting marshal, George?"

"No. But this is what we've come here for today," Crimond said, "to decide what's to be done, once an' for all, about Troy, an' who's going to have to do it."

"The council itself," said Hawtrey, who had been giving it careful thought, "along with concerned citizens, might

159

have to go there as a group, seeing there *is* no marshal." He looked at Crimond, then around at the sombre faces. "This here has got to be the last meeting about it," he said, "because talk alone isn't about to put this right. We have to take action."

By one after another it was affirmed. Joint action and without delay, before something else violent happened on account of Charlie Troy.

9

EYEGLASSES glinting, Vern Likens, his button-to-the-neck white coat arguably the most pristine garment to be seen in all of Gabriel, had been speaking in his quiet, assured voice to Brad and Mary Purnell, while looking out at the damp street. The window of the drugstore was fogged up but Likens had rubbed a small clear patch.

"Well now," he said then, "I don't know where they've all taken themselves off to now, but I do know they haven't yet gone up to Cavan's."

"Then you weren't at the meeting?" Mary asked.

"Me? At the meeting? No. Oh no. I'll not be a part of all that," Likens said. "But I sure heard all about it from Mrs Hawtrey." He dipped his head slightly, looking over the rims of his eyeglasses at Mary. "A friend of yours, I fancy? Mrs Hawtrey?"

"Yes." Mary could have said a great deal more but felt she did not wish to traverse all the latter-day complications that had become entangled with that friendship.

"Mm-m," said Likens. "It's really not my place to comment, of course, Mrs Purnell, but today Mrs Hawtrey's manner did strike me as a mite sad. What can I say? Er . . . withdrawn, uncertain. Yes, uncertain. Not her usual style at all, I thought. Almost as though she might have wanted to say much more to me than she did say. For some reason she couldn't bring herself to do it."

"But she was sure about that meeting?" Purnell asked. "I mean about what was said there; about their intentions?"

"Oh, absolutely," said Likens. "No question about that. Sometime soon they're going to head on up there *en masse*, confront Mr Troy and so on."

"No doubt they'll all be upset about what happened to Mr Kettley," said Mary, "above everything else."

Almost with passion, yet managing to maintain his professional control, Likens said at once, "Abe Kettley surely had to be a special kind of fool, that's my opinion, anyway. If he intended going anywhere near Mr Troy, then in all the circumstances it would have been prudent to do it in daylight." Likens partly lifted his pale, soft hands and let them fall again, a gesture that said as eloquently as anything could, that the episode had been beyond his comprehension. "I'm a peaceful man, or I like to believe that I am, maybe because I see all too often, at close quarters, the dreadful outcomes of violence." He waved one of the pallid hands vaguely towards a double-barrelled 12-gauge of ancient manufacture which was propped in a corner of the shop, a weapon, he had once told Purnell, accepted in payment for services rendered, though the exact nature of the dire circumstances surrounding that transaction, he had not specified. "There have been times," he said, "when I could have taken up that gun over there, and believe me I could use such things when I was a young fellow up in Michigan, against perfectly innocent wild-life, and confronted some of our more offensive citizens. If I chose to do it now, it would be to stand in front of some of these meeting-holding people and order them all away to conduct their own affairs and leave a dying man with dignity, and his child to bide here in peace."

Never before had Purnell known the mild, undemonstrative druggist to react in such a way. It revealed the depth of his feelings in the Troy affair, and hearing it somehow strengthened Purnell's own resolve.

"I can well understand that," Purnell said.

Likens shot him a sharp, tilt-headed look. "Will you hear any more of the

Voller matter? Is there to be a public hearing? Or about that drunken fool Hackman?"

Purnell shook his head vaguely. "I've heard nothing and as far as I know, Charlie Troy's heard nothing either." He could see that Likens was certainly up with the play. It had in fact crossed Purnell's own mind that charges might even be laid as part of the town's pressure on Troy and on anyone who was seen to be supporting him.

Because she had always respected Vern Likens and trusted him, Mary wanted him to know all that had taken place, so she then quietly told the druggist what had happened to young Imogen Troy at the hands of Ed Voller.

"Her father doesn't even know that," Mary said, "for the child was afraid to tell him, afraid of him trying to find the man and over-reaching his strength. But when the right opportunity comes, I shall tell Mr Troy, now that this man Voller is dead. But it did trouble

Imogen, that she's kept something back from her father. She told our boy that it went against a rule they'd shared, *Hide nothing.* It's been part of their survival."

Likens' mild face tautened and his eyes seemed to glitter behind the steel-rimmed discs. He walked a restless pace or two away, came back, then slapped a palm hard down on the worn counter. "Any of that town council know about that? Does Hawtrey? Does Crimond?"

"No."

"Be that as it may," said Likens, taking a breath, settling down again, "they must simply learn to leave this man alone. He's ill. He's very ill. Oh, while he's here I can carry on giving him morphine to hold off his pain, but he's weak and he tires easily. And of course there's the little girl to be considered." Clearly Likens was much disturbed by this whole situation, his reserve showing distinct signs of cracking.

"When are they likely to move?" Purnell asked.

Likens used the heel of one hand to make the clear patch on the window bigger. "Not yet awhile. Mrs Hawtrey said they'll wait 'til the little girl gets home from school."

Mary Purnell's face flushed with quick anger, but it was anger that was by no means directed towards Likens. "Can we be sure they won't just take her out of Annie's classroom or grab her in the alley? After all, she's been grabbed before by at least one grown man."

"Mrs Purnell," said Likens, "believe me I do know how you feel. There are times when I myself feel deeply ashamed of this community of ours, but day to day I have to go about my business in a place where there is no doctor, no other druggist, and try not to interfere in civic affairs." Now he looked soberly at Purnell. "To be honest, I'm not all that much use in . . . confrontations. Never been my style. I don't know how much use I might be, or more to the point, how much of a liability, but if you should come to believe at any time that my help might be of some value, then tell me. In saying that," he added, "I take it that you've got no intention of abandoning Mr Troy, even in the face of these developments today."

"I don't intend abandoning Mr Troy," Purnell said. He did not dismiss out of hand, either, any notion of help from Vern Likens who was, after all, a respected man in Gabriel, one who might well be seen by many people as neutral in the matter. Likens' voice, in the end, might be heeded, if not by the likes of Hawtrey or Crimond, then by others less certain of the morality in what was apparently to take place. "If I think there's any way that you can help," Purnell said, "I'll be at your door."

Back at their own house Mary was setting about preparing some food for the Troys, but she was still most unsettled and it showed. Purnell for the moment sat in silence, observing her.

By now, Purnell felt sure that news of the outcome of the second meeting at the mercantile would have permeated through Gabriel, and unless he was much mistaken there would be some shabby elements, those more often to be found in dumps like the Longhorn, who would be well disposed towards joining an upsurge of public protest. Purnell knew how swiftly such affairs could deteriorate, so that what had started out as a group of concerned townsmen could quite soon become no better than a lynch mob. He doubted the ability of either Hawtrey or Crimond to prevent matters getting out of hand in such a way, for in some men the vigilante instinct was not buried very deeply.

Mary clattered some plates down onto a sideboard with more than usual noise.

"If any of them *dare* lay a hand on that little girl — "

"Take it easy," Purnell advised,

holding up a hand. "Nobody's on the move yet. To me, Main looked about as lively as a wet graveyard. Right now they'll all be behind doors getting themselves prepared, getting in the right frame of mind, maybe even waiting for the next man to make the first move, watching through their windows."

She would not be so easily placated though.

"Brad, it's no good, I have to *do* something."

"What? Do what?"

She shook her head. "I don't know ... I — " Abruptly she broke off and went out of the room, peeling off her apron, but quite soon she reappeared and she was wearing her hooded, purple cloak.

"Mary, exactly what is it you think you can do?"

"What I ought to have done days ago. I'm going on down to say a word or two to Mabel Hawtrey, and when I've done with her I'm going to seek out Phena Crimond, and I'll leave neither of them in any doubt what *I* think. And I want to find out if they can look me right in the eye while I'm doing it."

"It can't do any good, Mary, not now. They're too afraid of their men."

"No? Well, so be it. But any use or no use, that's what I'm going to do. I won't *feel* right until I've said what I've got to say and I'm going to hand them out a warning about Imogen."

When, right after school was out, Rob Purnell walked Imogen home, he did not go in the house but he could see that all was quiet. As he walked away the only thing he noticed in particular was where, in recent times, the soft earth had been cut up by the passage of wheels, mute evidence of the traffic of wounding and death.

When he reached his own home it was to discover that his father was not there but had gone down to Wells Fargo on the off-chance of picking up some work there, and that his mother, cloaked to go out, was looking anxious but in a way excited, asking at once about Imogen.

"She's at home, I walked her to her house just like you said."

"All right, Rob. It's all right. I looked for you both after school was out but I must have missed you. Rob, you go right back down to Cavan's again and fetch Imogen here and stay with her until I get back or your pa comes in. Tell Mr Troy I'll be up there myself very soon." When the boy hesitated, seemed even set to ask questions, she waved her hands towards him in a shooing motion. "Just *go*, Rob . . . "

The boy hesitated no more but ran out and eventually headed up the trail on his errand. Soon after, Mary herself left the Purnell house and when Rob returned with the girl the place was deserted, seeming hollow and in some strange way, eerie.

Imogen had been nervous and had not wanted to leave her father but the yellow-skinned man, looking kindly on both of them, had urged her to go with

Rob. Whatever the need, he would find out from Mary soon.

"Rob's ma will no doubt have a good reason, Immy. Why not just do as she's asked? Remember, you can *trust* her. You can trust Rob."

Now, knowing that something very unusual must surely be about to happen, they were at one of the Purnell's upstairs windows, the girl still in the blue cape that Mary had given her, and looking out over the wet roof-tops. From where they were standing they could see a part of the street where the Purnell house stood, but beyond the roofs, only small slices of Main; yet there did not appear to be much activity of any sort there.

Time passed. They watched, feeling a strange tension. At one moment Imogen thought she had glimpsed two women walking quickly on Main, crossing between buildings, one of them wearing a purple cloak just like Rob's ma, but when the boy looked they had vanished and did not reappear.

After a while, seeing nothing more and hearing nothing, the boy said, "Whatever's goin' on, we'll find out all about it when Ma gets back. It's too cold here. Let's go down and sit near the stove."

She did not move immediately, but said, "That man who was shot . . . who was killed, he was the leather-leggings man."

"Yeah. His name was Voller."

"Pa says that's going to bring us some real trouble."

"But it was *my* pa that shot him, an' that was after Mr Kettley got wounded."

"Oh, my pa isn't blaming yours. It's just that things have happened in other places because of who my pa is — who he *was*. A lot of real nasty things seem to happen to us, Rob, wherever we go. But my pa, he's a good man. He didn't do half of the things they say he did."

"Pa reckons people get afraid of what *might* happen — afraid for themselves, that's mostly what it is."

"Look!" The girl was pointing and there was urgency in the way the word came out.

Rob had moved away but quickly came back to the window. "What?"

"On Main. There. And there. Men on buggies, a buckboard. Where are they all going, Rob? Look there's another . . . and another. Rob I don't like it. What's happening? Are they going to hurt my pa?" Her sooty eyes were wide and she was as near to panic as he had seen her.

Rob could only shake his head in bewilderment. "Don't know, Immy." The boy slipped into using her father's pet name for her and she raised no objection. "Whatever it is, we can't do anything. Just trust my ma. C'mon now, downstairs where it's warmer."

Somewhat reluctantly the girl, very tense and pale, followed him.

Vern Likens, in his doorway, saw the mud-churning buggies going by, the heavily-coated, serious men riding on them, all heading along Main from a place of assembly near Hawtrey's mercantile and out along the trail towards Cavan's.

After they had passed by, not even a dog was stirring on the wet street.

10

NEARLY a dozen buggies and some buckboards were on the move, the men aboard them coated against the chill, not far to go but keeping their boots dry for as long as possible.

There was little talk now, no calling between vehicles. The assembly outside the mercantile, maybe three dozen men in all, had been vocal, even enthusiastic; now there was an atmosphere of sober resolution, of having gone beyond a point at which they might have turned back.

Too many of their fears had now acquired dreadful substance; the sole peace-keeper wounded, not badly, yet only a small measure away from something that might have seen him on Edlin's table; two dead, both persons of no great moral account, yet who had been drawn, foolishly as it turned out, by the very presence of Charlie Troy. And because men of their unappealing stripe had tried, so would others.

They were not hurrying, the horses plodding along the squelching trail, laden vehicles creaking, coats being soiled with spatters of mud. Misty rain was drifting across now, hazing the way ahead, but the men could now see the dilapidated house and its sorry-looking outbuildings and the dark trees clumped nearby.

Some of those making this approach were armed with a variety of pistols, these being carried out of sight under coats, and at least one had a sawn-off shotgun so concealed. Even George Crimond had a .41 calibre Hammond Bulldog usually kept in a drawer at his freight office, a lady's pistol, surely, yet affording him an absurd sense of security.

Hawtrey, on the leading buggy, now raised a hand and called, his voice flattened, diminished by the outdoors, so that when his buggy halted, some others whose reinsmen had not heard the call came steadily on and finished by hauling up urgently, in some disarray, one turned at right-angles.

Hawtrey surveyed the wheel-cut approaches to the house, a poor structure of broken windows and sagging eaves, lying silently in the light rain, grey on a grey afternoon. Even Hawtrey, a man of no overt sensibilities, looked upon the wet, age-raddled building as not unsymbolic of their purpose here today, no animation about it and no joy in it. The sooner the business was done, the better. Flicking the reins, not even glancing at George Crimond on the seat beside him or at the pair of coldly-miserable citizens seated behind him, he set the buggy forward again. All the vehicles had cleared the trail by the time the big, rocking Concord from Shearman and points south-east went churning by, a loaded coach, boxes piled high, pressing on to Gabriel and a pause there of thirty minutes.

In Gabriel Purnell had come away from Wells Fargo and was crossing a rutted Main to where Vern Likens was standing, white-coated, in his doorway.

"They're away," said Likens, eyeglasses glinting, "buggies and buckboards. Just gone."

"Talked themselves into it at last," Purnell murmured. Wearing a denim jacket, a shell-belt and his Smith and Wesson pistol and black, shallow-crowned hat, his boots were generously larded with street mud. "I'd planned to go there earlier than this, but got delayed over yonder. I'm going now."

Likens checked his move away, saying, "Young feller came by who'd been up at the mercantile. He claimed that some of them were armed. Under their coats."

Purnell held the druggist's gaze a moment, then went clumping away along the greasy boardwalk.

At Cavan's, Hawtrey secured the reins and stepped down into deep, wet grass, Crimond and his other passengers following him. Soon everyone was down, standing uncertainly near the heads of the vapouring horses, many with that odd, hunched attitude common to those enduring fine rain. There was some uncertainty about the next move, whether to make their presence known now or approach the house.

Hawtrey solved that; he cupped cold fingers to his mouth. "Troy! Charlie Troy!"

At first it seemed that his calling was to produce no result. Then Hawtrey's jaw fell, and Crimond's alongside him, as slowly a number of figures came into view from around the back of the house, moving one by one through the wet grass, eventually to stand ranged along the frontage, fifteen, no maybe twenty, some holding umbrellas, others in hooded cloaks, the bright colours of these seeming brighter in the dull daylight, some women of Gabriel.

Mary Purnell, was there in her purple cloak, Mabel Hawtrey with an umbrella, Phena Crimond in a dark red cloak, Annie Walenski in her dowdy coat and unadorned, wet straw hat; and Ada Meares too, small, tentative, and others, ordinary wives, standing quietly in the rain facing the men and horses and buggies drawn up some forty feet away.

"What's this?" asked Hawtrey. "What's going on here?"

Phena Crimond turned her head to look at one of the others, and Mabel Hawtrey, apparently spurred by the sidelong glance, said in a surprisingly firm voice, "Henry, this man is not to be turned out of here. We want you all to let him be. This is not the way." When she had finished she seemed a touch short of breath but appeared to be no less determined.

"*Not the way?*" Hawtrey's long face was gaining colour high on his cheekbones. "*Not the way?* What in the name of God are you saying, woman?"

"I'm talking — " Mabel Hawtrey's firm voice now for the first time faltered but she took a fresh breath, " — talking about what you and those men at your back have clearly come here to do."

An unidentifiable voice from among the men called, "They don't know what they're at, Henry. Let's git on by an' do it."

Mary Purnell now came a half pace forward and called, "Who was that?" When there was no reply she called again, "Who was that?" when there was still no answer, Mary said, "Whoever it was, if he can manage to work up the courage he'll be the first to break the line, for that's what will have to be done to get through to Mr Troy."

Horses were wagging heads, blowing, shifting, flicking ears, leather was creaking and from time to time there was the clink of metal. Men were moving around restlessly, swishing through the grass, most tending to look towards Hawtrey who, throughout this entire affair, from the precincts of the mercantile to this sorry place, had always had the most to say.

But it was George Crimond who now came to the fore, perhaps wishing to be seen, belatedly, as asserting his authority here, taking a firm civic stand. "Now, all you ladies, just listen to me. As the elected chief citizen, I can speak for the Gabriel town council. A council decision *has* been made that Mr Troy must be asked to leave. I'm not about to go into all of the reasons for that, because they're already known well enough; but that decision has been made and we cannot stand by and see it unmade by those who are not of the elected council."

It would have sounded much more convincing if, having started out boldly in the same voice he used while campaigning for votes, he had been able to finish in the same style instead of allowing the volume to fall away. It was perhaps why Mabel Hawtrey said immediately:

"And if we still refuse to move?"

Crimond moistened his lips, his pouchy face sickly in the dull daylight, for after all this was Henry Hawtrey's wife challenging him, not just some anonymous little woman; but he had to stick to his position. "Then, Mrs Hawtrey, we'll have no option but to move on through."

Mary Purnell said, "You'll drive over us?"

An awkward, loaded silence fell over the wet, unhappy scene. Phena Crimond spoke, and though she did not raise her voice unduly, what she said was clear enough to be heard by every man and woman there. "Does that mean that, if need be, you would raise your *hands* to us?" Though fine rain was still from time to time drifting across, she had allowed the hood of her deep red cloak to fall back against her shoulders. No thick layer of powder was on her face today and though the bruise on her cheekbone had faded slightly, an odd mark was still visible there. It could not be certain that many of those present were particularly aware of it, but when Crimond's eyes shifted uncomfortably, suddenly he discovered that Mary Purnell was looking at him with a contempt so thinly veiled that the message it sent him was inescapable. "*She knows.*" Crimond looked away, seeming to shrink in size, his round head sinking back into his collar like a tortoise withdrawing into its shell. If Mary Purnell knew, then how many others might?

The wetness and the clammy chill was beginning to work upon those who had come out on the buggies and there occurred now a shifting of the men, a tighter grouping, water dripping from hats, faces raw. A bull-necked man, Drummond, a teamster who had no wife among these women, came up level with Hawtrey and Crimond.

"Henry, I didn't come here to be mouthed down by a bundle o' petticoats that ought to be home wipin' little asses." As Drummond's long coat moved he could be seen to be the one holding a sawn-off 10-gauge, pointing downwards next to his right leg.

Though it was not Hawtrey who started the move, others, heartened by Drummond's bold statement, also came forward, causing some small show of uncertainty among the women. But Mary stilled it.

"Don't move. Don't break the line. Stay facing them." As the men, Hawtrey and Crimond heading them, continued moving forward, she said, "You'll need to put your whips to us. Who'll be the first?"

The men's advance faltered, then stopped, though not entirely through this defiance.

Troy was out.

It was the first time that any of these men had set eyes on him and an utter silence fell as he came walking slowly along the side of the house, moving as would someone bare-footed and avoiding sharp stones. When he arrived at the front corner of the house he stopped, one skinny hand placed against the wet boards for support.

He regarded them out of eyes that

were dark pits, his face yellowed vellum stretched over bone, his upper teeth just visible, his lips nearly colourless, his clothes hanging on what had become a skeletal body. Perhaps because it no longer fitted well, he was wearing no hat, and his hair, once dark, could be seen to be speckled with grey and receding from the front. Troy had brought no pistol out with him.

Some of the women looked at him anxiously, then just as quietly brought their attention back to the men. All but one. Ada Meares, moving across to Charlie Troy, because of her short stature had to reach up at full stretch to hold an umbrella over him and only partially over herself. Among the assembled men, her husband, his mouth open, now wanted to be anywhere but where he was.

What Troy had to say in a voice that today was not strong, he said to the women, but they did not for an instant shift their attention away from those facing them.

"I've got no wish to see anybody hurt here," said Troy slowly. "Ladies, I don't have any idea what to say to you, except to offer you thanks, but I ask (he took a couple of short breaths, looked down, then up again and went deliberately on) I ask you to take no more risks on my account."

But these women out here in the misty rain had come as far as they had with tight-lipped resolution after they had listened to what Mary Purnell had had to say to them, and with every passing minute, even in soggy discomfort, not one among them would have even considered retreating one step. It was as though they had, singly and in this united band, at some point crossed an invisible boundary and had found existence on the far side so filled with new possibilities that none now wished to recross, to relinquish ground that had been gained in matters which went far beyond this single affair of Charlie Troy. It was appropriate, therefore, that it was not Mary Purnell but Mabel Hawtrey who said then:

"We've got no intention of giving way, Mr Troy. We're all of a mind about it. Not only for your sake but for your little girl's, now that everything has come out."

Purnell, having seen the stage roll into Gabriel, had arrived quietly, virtually unnoticed, standing back near the horses. A few other men had come drifting in, swelling the group now confronting Troy and the Gabriel women, and the last of these to arrive said in a voice loud enough to be heard all over:

"Stage come in from Shearman, an' it ain't good news."

Cold faces swung to him.

"What's happened?" Hawtrey asked.

"It ain't what's happened, it's what could be comin'. Jack French, he's been seen in Shearman, him an' two more, name o' Dave Dimond an' some other rooster . . . Pepper? No, Pepperill."

Troy had been looking down. Slowly his head came up.

What had been said caused an immediate swell of cross-talk but Hawtrey raised his voice above it. "Well, that's it, boys, what we've been talking about all along. There's no way we want that animal French anywhere near Gabriel."

Some of the women now began looking at each other. Unhurriedly, Purnell had been walking forward and was now standing level with Hawtrey but five yards to one side. Nearest him was Drummond with the 10-gauge.

Troy was speaking again and it was almost uncanny how his laboured, quiet words were being heard. "I can't pretend that Jack French (a breath-drawing pause) that Jack French won't have got to know where I am. Shearman's too close to Gabriel for it to be just chance. So I've got to agree that it's only a matter of time before he comes here, maybe not much time at that." Again he stopped, breathing as though drawing on a bank of breath which was close to running out. "I can't

191

wait around an' see that happen, an' maybe have other people shot." Those close to him could see that sweat was slick on his forehead. "So you'll get what you want."

Phena Crimond, beyond Ada Meares the next closest to Troy, suddenly said, "No. No, that's just not possible." She extended a gloved hand. "Just look at this man! To send him away in this state, in this weather, with only a child to help him would be the same as *us* putting a pistol to him. Can't you all *see* that?"

Drummond, his thick neck reddening, shouted, "He says he wants to go, let 'im go!" As he spoke, Drummond took a step forward, his coat swinging open, the 10-gauge now visible to people who might not have been aware of it earlier. No doubt Troy saw it too, but it drew not the slightest change of expression from him.

Purnell, however, was not content about the cut-down shotgun. "Break the gun," he said to Drummond, "an' unload it. This is no place for it."

Drummond, now the focus of attention, was first impelled to bluster but at the same time he had no real desire to cross Purnell. Yet he did resist. "It's not ag'in my rights to carry it, Purnell."

"Before all these ladies here, because of why they've come here, it's now offensive, so break it an' unload it."

"You can't come here demanding anything, Purnell!" This was Hawtrey of course, very pale and agitated, clearly angry and frustrated over the way things had gone, still appalled by the presence of his own wife among these women and now deeply resentful of interference by Purnell.

Purnell ignored Hawtrey, moving a pace nearer Drummond. The bull-necked man was still glaring at him, but capitulated, broke the shotgun, withdrew the red, brass-capped cartridge which he shoved in a pocket, closed the gun and concealed it under his coat out of the wet.

"That's better," Purnell commented, then raising his voice a trifle, said, "All other weapons being carried had best be kept where they are, out of sight."

A few heads went down, Crimond's among them, when he said that.

And through all this, Crimond had been staring a lot at his wife, who had been staring back at him unflinchingly. Now he was able to contain himself no longer, yet it was in a tone of genuine puzzlement that he asked, "Why, Phena? Why *you* in all this?" There was a complete absence of aggression, for Crimond, in his heart, knew that what there was between him and his wife had to an extent been publicly exposed.

"It's for that young girl," Phena Crimond said. "For Imogen's sake as much as for Mr Troy's. Did you know that Voller caught her not fifty yards from where you're standing, on her way home? Did you know that he *touched* her? Did you know that with Mr Troy gone — if Voller or that dreadful cowboy, Hackman, had shot him — Voller would have . . . have wanted her for himself? Do you even *care* about the things that go on in this community anyway?"

Their faces were like masks, all staring fixedly at mild Mrs Phena Crimond, her hood still cast back, her hair wet, her face with the strange little bluish mark on it.

Finally Hawtrey, some of the fire having gone out of him, asked almost bemusedly, "You're suggesting he'd have killed Mr Troy for that . . . purpose?"

Purnell spoke up. "Only partly. The first time Ed Voller came here with Hackman, I know for sure he'd been given whiskey-money to rid Gabriel of the risks of (smiling sourly) the risks of the plague coming. The little girl wasn't the first reason. She was the bonus."

"That's a damn' outrage!" Hawtrey shouted, but soon demonstrated that he was not referring to the issue of morality. "You're trying to tell us that somebody in this town handed money to Ed Voller, to a drifter, I won't say *rancher*, to a drunkard, and sent him to shoot Troy?"

"Yes," Purnell said, "I am."

"Who? Tell us then, Purnell. Who?"

"Ed Voller wasn't quite gone when I got to him. He gave me a name."

"Whose name?"

"You'd best put the question to your acting marshal."

A stunned silence fell.

"Impossible!" Hawtrey snapped. But brother-in-law Crimond looked down, saying nothing in Kettley's defence. It was all moving too quick for Crimond.

"While you're at it, ask him his reasons," Purnell suggested. "But I'd guess it was all about seeking office. Some go to any lengths to get it." Now he looked at George Crimond. "An' some that get into public office can show a face that's not always the real one." Purnell then raised his voice so that there could be no possible misunderstanding. "Charlie Troy, here, will go nowhere until he's fit to drive the wagon or he can make other arrangements. Right now he's going back in the house an' take a spell. Imogen won't be here, she'll be with my wife." Mary nodded gently. "But *I'll* be here. If French does come, then I'll stand with Charlie, who's broken no law in the past, or now, an' who's defended the peace himself, in his time."

Someone, mercifully someone buried in the crowd, called, "What about that Fielding woman, the one that got burned?"

Troy's skull-like face lifted again, no more than a yellowish mask, seeking the speaker, but it was Purnell who repeated in his hard voice, *"Broken no law in the past, or now."* And to the other men, "My best advice is that from now on you keep whoever said that real quiet, an' you an' him clear right out of here now." Some were truly taken aback for such a look was on Purnell's face as they had never seen before, and it was chilling. Of all those standing there in that bleak afternoon perhaps only Charlie Troy himself knew the truth about such a look, and seeing it, even felt a momentary tug of hope, yet a kind of dread at the same time. "An' my last piece of advice is for all you boys to go back into Gabriel afoot, an' let these ladies ride." Purnell turned from them and at once drew Mary aside. "Tell Vern Likens I'll be there soon, to call in his offer."

Whatever bluster there had been among the men of Gabriel had now given way to something else, a hollow fear. They began dispersing, no bold words now, and little talk of any sort.

★ ★ ★

The Cavan place now lay quiet in the early evening as though the day's events had never been. The rain had ceased and Troy had rested. Purnell had visited Gabriel, gone first to his house to reassure Imogen, then to the drugstore to talk urgently with Vern Likens.

To Troy, he said now, "If French shows up on the doorstep on his way from Shearman, we'll have to take our chances as they come. If he shows up in town first, and Vern Likens sees him and gets to hear about him, we'll get a warning, the few minutes that might make the difference."

For acknowledgement Troy merely moved his head slightly, closing his eyes and opening them again. Then quietly, as far as it was possible in this situation to make plans, they made some. Presently and after a long silence, Troy said, "The house fire all that time ago, it's true that the woman, Bella Fielding, got burned to death in it, an' true it got started accidentally by one of my men; but it's not true she was just . . . left in there. Tried real hard to get to her, Brad, but the fire spread too fast, was too fierce. Never felt such heat." Troy waited a while, breathing shallowly. "We'd gone in there on word that had come to us about French, that turned out to be all shit. Oh, we did some things wrong, an' that's down to me. But faced with the same (gasping a little) situation, I'd go in hard again, like we did then. You can always be wiser, after."

"Belle Fielding. She was French's cousin?"

Troy's ravaged face twisted in the travesty of a smile. "Yeah. *Close* cousin." Then: "A lot o' things in this world ain't what you an' me might think of as natural." Plainly that led him to other thoughts and when he looked up at Purnell the other man could see the deep hurt that was there. "Voller. She was right, y'know Brad, as young as she is. If I'd known I would've tried to find the bastard an' blow his breakfast through his asshole." Again he paused. "But French, well, I've always known that one o' these fine days he'd get a sniff of where I was, but by God, I did want to get Immy safe away before it happened.

Then it wouldn't have mattered a spit in hell." He looked down at the floor, made a small shrugging movement as though physically tired, and tired, too, of being so much on the move, but he still looked like a man who had glimpsed other dangerous fires, and just as fleetingly they were reflected in his sunken eyes. "I know it's said I bring a goddamn' plague." Presently he fell asleep in the chair.

Purnell fetched a blanket and covered him.

Purnell himself slept fitfully, half afraid of allowing weariness to wear at him, half afraid of sleeping too soundly and not hearing a signal.

In the morning Purnell went into the yard and looked at the cloudy sky above where Gabriel lay, a haze of early woodsmoke hanging all across it. He went back inside. Charlie Troy was coming stiffly awake.

About an hour after Purnell had stood briefly in the Cavan yard, Vern Likens in his drugstore wiped quickly at clouded glass the better to see out onto the street.

Three men had emerged from a cafe and were now approaching the tie-rail where three horses stood, sturdy and well-travelled animals by their looks, mud-spattered, with bed-rolls up behind the cantles.

One man changed his mind and strolled away into the mouth of an alley where he stood pissing steamily, and presently, rebuttoning, rejoined his companions. They seemed in no great hurry to go anywhere, one of them building a quirly, then bending over, lighting it, blue smoke wafting thinly in the cold air.

Tall men they were, all three wearing leather leggings over cord pants, canvas brush-jackets and battered, wide-brimmed hats with leather thongs hanging loose, all slung with thick shell-belts and armed with pistols, a scabbarded rifle on only one of the horses.

Likens, behind his glass, was straining

to see them clearly, wiping at his spyhole patch again with a piece of gauze bandage. From Troy, Purnell had gained a fair description of Jack French and in turn had given it to Likens. And now here the man was, darkish skin, dark sideburns to his jawbone, his cheeks severely pockmarked, a man over six feet tall. Likens had no doubt whatsoever that this was French.

And Dimond too, almost as tall. "*Used to have a thin black moustache.*" Yes. And the slightly younger one — for French and Dimond would be in their late forties — Pepperill, with the stringy appearance and the gold-mottled skin of a red-head.

Now they were exchanging a few words with a passer-by, a boy from Lowe's grain store, Likens thought, who was pointing now along Main.

Likens did not wait to see any more. "*Please God I'll be in time.*" In the back-room of the drugstore he took from shelves certain paper sacks, then went quickly back into the front with them, to where the pot-bellied stove was.

Across the street the men were mounting up, settling into saddles, blue smoke trailing from the one with the quirly.

In an odd, cracked voice, French murmured, "Well, I'll be god-damned! Come right on by where the prick was at."

The horses were brought shuffling away from the tie-rail and the riders began walking them up Main, line abreast.

11

MARY PURNELL, strength draining away from her limbs, knew as soon as she looked out a window at the louring morning sky that the time had come.

The children were sitting at breakfast, engrossed in their easy talk, Rob, as he had from the beginning, finding Imogen Troy an agreeable companion, of less serious mind now than she had sometimes been, and much happier to appear each day at Annie Walenski's school. Some pupils there still tended to hold back — perhaps because of what was being said at home — but at least she was now free to come and go in safety, and that because no-one else had any desire to tangle with Rob Purnell. Opinion was that if big Dave Schiller, even with help, could not handle Purnell, then who else would stand a chance? And Annie Walenski was keeping a hawkish eye on proceedings, liking the girl, and had said to Mary, "It's hard to believe she's missed so much school. She's a bright little girl."

Mary came to the table and when they saw the expression on her face their chattering subsided for they knew that something was badly amiss. Before the questions began, Mary said, "Now listen to me, both of you. You won't be going to school. You'll stay with me and keep inside the house."

Eyes clouding, Imogen said, "It's my pa, isn't it? Something about my pa?" She would have got off her chair but Mary checked her.

"Immy, as far as I know, your pa is all right. Mr Purnell is still with him. You're not to worry, no matter what you might hear. Do you understand? Rob, you too?"

"Yeah." His expression said something else.

Imogen, though, had been travelling

a highly dangerous trail with Charlie Troy long enough to have become well aware why, sometimes, they had had to douse a camp-fire in a hurry or turn a lamp down and sit utterly still in heart-pounding silence, listening for footfalls, or grasp a door-latch, muffling it, stepping out of some seedy overnight hotel into sweet, velvet, anonymous darkness.

"That man's come here, hasn't he? That Jack French?"

"I believe he has, Imogen." She took the girl's small, soft hands in her own. "Don't worry. Don't try to go up there, little love. Truly it would only make things worse. Trust me. Trust Rob's pa, who'll be there and who'll do his best." *Who, in the next ten minutes, might lie dead alongside Charlie Troy*. The thought was searing agony, like a knife sliding into her.

Rob asked, "How can you know he's here, Ma?"

Mary said, "Both of you, get up

from the table quietly and come to the window."

In the streets of Gabriel, those who were abroad had now stopped whatever they were doing and were staring open-mouthed. Small groups formed, people asking each other what in the name of God it could be.

Down at the Cavan place, Purnell, he and Charlie Troy having eaten — Troy most sparingly, for breakfast had become a meal which he could not always keep down — was still leaning in the porch doorway carrying on a casual conversation, when suddenly Purnell saw it and chopped abruptly into something Troy was starting to say.

"Charlie. Time's come."

Grunting, Troy came slowly from the chair and walked to where he, too, could see. Today he had Ed Voller's old shell-belt bandoliered over one shoulder, the heavy loads looking outlandishly substantial against his sunken chest. The Forehand and Wadsworth .44 pistol was still in his chair where it had lain the night through near his emaciated thigh. The second pistol, taken from Voller, the Remington, lay on a shelf.

No double thump of Likens' 12-gauge, however, had disturbed the dark hours, for that was to have been the night-signal if any such could be made, a poor arrangement at best, both Purnell and Likens had agreed, but marginally better than no arrangement at all.

But now the daytime signal was overpowering the blue gauze of woodsmoke that seemed eternally to be smeared over Gabriel. Rolling up through that smoke into the leaden overcast, from what would be the drugstore's pipe chimney, was smoke of a vastly different kind, smoke generated by chemicals flung onto the stove by Likens, and it was this that was stopping Gabriel people in their tracks and what Mary Purnell had seen and recognized for what it was, and what Rob and Imogen, at a window, open-mouthed, were seeing at this moment.

No thin, insipid blue, this smoke but, pluming strongly away, a smoke so thick that it seemed almost to have substance to it, at one moment deep crimson, at the next, bright yellow, these startling colours spreading out gradually as they dissipated to become part of the vaporous covering over Gabriel.

During their slow ride, in their wide-ranging surveillance, the three horsemen who lately had quit the end of Main and were on the muddy trail through green brush that would lead them to the house they sought, saw it too, and so unusual was the sight that all three drew rein, the horses wagging heads and stepping sideways as their riders sat staring back, pondering its significance.

The ginger-haired man, Pepperill, drew on his quirly, took it briefly from his lips and blew an urgent stream of smoke of his own out into the damp, cold atmosphere. Dimond sat sucking noisily at his terrible teeth, trying to dislodge a fibre of bacon. Jack French sat, swarthy, still-faced, gloved hands resting on the saddlehorn.

After a few moments Pepperill spat out a scrap of tobacco and remarked, "Mebbe they got around to burnin' some o' the old whores."

Dimond abandoned his probing for the vagrant fragment of bacon. "Dump like this couldn't afford to waste no whores, even old 'uns."

French gave the phenomenon one final look, then hauled his mount around and walked it on, Dimond following, then Pepperill, but from time to time all three glanced back at the cap of coloured smoke piling over the rooftops.

When they arrived at a place from which they could view the battered frontage of Cavan's, standing in utter stillness, they looked down, too, at many recent wheel-ruts and evidence of the passage of numerous horses.

"For a place that looks empty," French remarked, "it gits to see a whole lot o' visitors." He glanced at Dimond, eyebrows raised.

Dimond reached back and unscabbarded his rifle and the sound of its loading-action was sharply metallic in the morning as he worked the lever to chamber a round. Pepperill flicked the sad remains of his quirly into long wet grass.

All three walked their horses a few yards closer and stopped again. French nodded. Dimond, muttering to his horse which was inclining to move restlessly beneath him, raised his rifle and sent a lashing shot through one of the broken windows, then had to apply himself to bringing the even more restive animal under control. When he had got it more or less settled, Dimond shot again, this time smashing a hitherto intact window, then slammed another loud shot into the front door. He levered again, then all three horsemen sat their mounts as though waiting for this sudden gunfire to produce some sort of result.

As minutes went silently by it became clear that it was not going to. One of French's hands, upraised, caused Dimond, getting set for another shot, to lower the rifle.

"We'll go take a look all around," French said; and to Dimond, "Stir the prick up as we go."

Nudging the horses forward through the long grass they soon saw grass that had been well trampled, obviously by a number of people. Pepperill and French drew their long pistols. They went on, Dimond in the lead, then French, then Pepperill, and slowly they circled the Cavan house which was standing as still as a Monday church, but every so often Dimond blasted a bullet through a window. French's eyes raked the outbuildings and the uncovered wagon standing near the barn. When they had made a complete circuit, Dimond sat thumbing fresh loads in through the side-slot of the rifle, reloading the magazine. French then nodded and they dismounted, each finding an arm of brush to which they light-hitched their mounts.

French now taking the lead, they went up onto the front porch and were able to observe at close quarters the hole that Dimond's recent bullet had made. French tried the door latch and somewhat to his surprise the door opened, though stiffly, but gave way fully when French thumped a boot to the base of it.

In Gabriel, Vern Likens, impatiently waving away questions about his chimney-smoke, went about, chiefly on Main, warning as many people as he could and asking them to pass it on. "*Keep off the streets*. If this fight that's coming should — God forbid — spill over into the town," Likens said, "we'll none of us be safe." Thereupon he despatched an eager youth to Annie Walenski to tell her to keep her charges inside the classroom until any shooting was all over, a message which Plain Annie received, arms folded, in straight-lipped silence. At least it answered one question in her mind, that as to where Imogen Troy and Rob Purnell had got to. Scarcely had the youth departed than she was chalking up on the blackboard in her faultless calligraphy, the verses of the morning's hymn, not quite apposite, but as close as Annie felt she could get; and before the messenger had regained the main street, the shrill, untutored choir could be heard in full voice.

"O God of love, O King of peace,
Make wars throughout the world
to cease;
The wrath of sinful men restrain,
Give peace, O God, give peace
again."

Quite soon the streets of Gabriel had been washed empty, this time not with rain, but with fear, for from the direction of the Cavan place had come the sharp, lashing sounds of rifle-shots.

Likens had gone hurrying to the

Purnell house where Mary, startled to see that the druggist, still in his white, buttoned-up coat, was carrying his shotgun, met him on the porch.

"Mrs Purnell, are the children with you?"

"Yes, upstairs, and there they'll be staying."

"Ah . . . yes. Yes. Well, it was just to be sure. I've put the word out and sent a message to Miss Walenski." Eyeglasses winking, looking around him, he did not seem to know what he ought to do next, having performed so many unusual tasks already today, and only now appearing to realize that he had brought his shotgun. "I don't know why I have this," he said. "I expect it made me feel better." He looked almost contrite. "I doubt I could use it in anger."

Mary smiled faintly but she was pale and very tense. "Thank you, Mr Likens, for coming."

Likens nodded jerkily and walked

216

away, an incongruous sight indeed, a small-town druggist with a double-barrelled shotgun, and she could have wept for him, this mild, scholarly, courteous man, with concerns for others, going armed for fear of truly terrible men, armed for such a purpose for the only time in his entire life. She thought it was as though he had not only wanted to *do* something on this awful day, but to *stand* for something as well, and silently she blessed him for it, and feared for him and for everybody.

Deep inside that part of the Cavan house still intact, putting boots to doors, they were yelling for Troy, knowing that he — or somebody — had been in here, for there were signs of habitation, not least the stove with bright embers in it and still giving off gentle heat.

About to head on out through the back porch to the yard, they heard horses on the move and whickering, and the men turned and ran back through the house, cursing yielding floorboards, and out the way they had come in.

Sure enough, their mounts were loose, spooked too, that was plain, all three heading for the Gabriel trail, though slowing now. Who had set them away they could not tell for there was no sign anywhere else of man or beast. To Pepperill, French said, "See if yuh can git to 'em without spookin' 'em again. Watch that bastard o' mine. He'll be fit to lash out."

Pepperill slid his pistol into its old, oily holster and walked gangle-footed down off the porch. A quietness had come down again.

"We'll take us another look around that yard. The bastard can't be far away." Yet French stood for another half minute watching, for Pepperill had reached a place where he must now pass from sight behind brush, the horses having wandered further away, also beyond view. Pepperill glanced back.

French called, "See 'em?" Pepperill nodded.

"Fifty yards." Pepperill gave a low whistle, clearly trying to entice his own horse, then passed from their view.

Pepperill, going carefully so as not to alarm the now standing, rein-trailing horse, was almost halfway to them when, maybe forty feet from him, Purnell came out from behind some juniper. Abruptly Pepperill stopped, his freckled face showing whitely in the steel-coloured morning. Whoever this bastard was, he was not Charlie Troy.

"Figured one of you would be bound to come for 'em," Purnell said, though not raising his voice. "By the looks of you, you're not Jack French, but if you're here for Charlie Troy, then I'm not *him*, either. But I'll have to do."

Pepperill was a capable enough man with the weapon he carried but generally he liked to know ahead of time what the true odds were, so it was the merest hesitation in the face of the unknown, before closing his hand on the butt of the old Colt, that cost him dear.

It was certainly true that he cleared the weapon away as fast as he had ever got it done, but the long barrel was only part way through its upward arc when Purnell's astonishing draw of the Smith and Wesson Army was already beyond that same stage, and Pepperill felt the unholy impact, like being struck by a swinging spade, at the same instant that a thunderclap smote his eardrums and the flick of flame and whip of gunsmoke seemed to imprint on his eyeballs.

Pepperill did not remember going down in the mud of the chopped-up trail, was not aware of the three startled horses going skittering away again, could not comprehend, when he tried to raise his head, that the dark object only inches from his face was a boot belonging to the tall, lazy-walking man who had shot him. And in the space of no more than four heartbeats,

Pepperill could not recall, either, who he himself was, and in the measure of another four, remembered nothing whatsoever.

French and Dimond were one on either side of the untidy yard, in a slow search of the outbuildings, Dimond in the act of pushing open a sagging, age-grey door with the muzzle of his rifle when the remote pistol-shot sounded.

At once Dimond came swishing to the middle of the yard, cursing suddenly, kicking at some scrap of concealed junk that he had struck a boot against. French turned where he was, pistol half extended, quite motionless now, listening, but there was no more shooting.

Dimond said, "Pepper's onto somethin'."

"Mebbe," said French, "mebbe." His dark, almost Hispanic face with its fiercely pitted skin looked as though it had set hard, his agate eyes wolfishly watchful, waiting for some sight or sound of Pepperill.

221

"Musta come on Troy," Dimond said, "an' got it done."

"Mebbe," said French, oddly unconvinced. There was something far from right about this whole place and it was only now that the significance of the strange, brightly-coloured smoke over Gabriel and this unsettling stillness here began connecting vaguely in French's mind. Having come confidently, seeking a man known to be in the extremities of a destroying disease, he had found only a house, decaying as his quarry was reputed to be, but no longer sheltering him. Jack French had boasted freely about one day coming up with Charlie Troy, and of late, when he had got wind of him, had heard that he had been seen on the move in a slow wagon, down to Shearman and beyond, and only a child with him, French had scented that opportunity afresh, a death-stench mixed with the smell of long-dead ashes.

Still Pepperill did not come.

"Ain't gonna look for 'ol Pepper 'til

we've given this dump the once-over," French said.

They moved towards the bulky barn, perhaps the least damaged structure of all, Dimond first stepping up to look in the wagon; then French, poking the long barrel of the pistol ahead of him, eased on inside. Dimond, rifle held angled across his chest, was leaning against the tail-gate of the wagon watching the sad yard and the sagging house at the other end of it and hoping for an early sight of Pepperill returning.

French, in the pungent, straw-littered gloom, had found the Troy horses, seeing that they had been provided with water and ample feed and that fresh straw had been put down. It occurred to French at this time that if Troy was as ill as had been suggested, then he had done well to look after these animals in this way. A child would have had difficulty in doing so French believed; which of course raised the possibility that Troy was being helped. The strong niggle of doubt that French had felt when Dimond had said, of Pepperill, "*Musta come on Troy an' got it done*," now came back more strongly. Pepperill had failed to reappear. French walked slowly on, eyes probing this way and that, finding no-one.

Outside, Dimond, straightening up from his negligent attitude at the wagon, blinked his eyes as though not quite believing that, from out of trees near the left side of the house and going painfully towards the front of it, was a thin figure, perhaps bandoliered with bullets, his clothing very loose on him, his back more or less towards Dimond and of course some distance from him.

Quickly Dimond brought the rifle up, yet even as his shot tore the silence, he had known at the instant of firing that the target had passed from view around the front of the building. Dimond levered in a fresh load, the spent case, ejecting, winking away in the dull light, then he began to go forward as fast as the long grass permitted, calling to French, "I *seen* the bastard!"

Still coming towards the back of the house, alert for any further sight of the man he was convinced was Troy, he thought — no, was sure — that he had glimpsed a figure at a window, there and gone. By this time Dimond was a mere few yards short of the back porch, pressing urgently ahead, determined that Troy was not to be allowed a second chance.

French, now out of the barn, saw Dimond go pounding up onto the porch and then, rifle held in both hands, his hat hanging by its thongs between his shoulders, vanish inside. French began running up the yard.

Dimond, yelling like a drunken Apache, was by that time bursting into the kitchen.

Charlie Troy, still recovering from his efforts of the past few minutes, having come in the front door, was sitting in the large, hide-covered chair, his body half turned, both of his own thin arms propped on one of the roundly-padded arms of the chair, and he was holding the Forehand and Wadsworth .44, his left hand supporting the right.

The blast of the discharge was inordinately loud in the enclosed room, the gunsmoke immediately copious and pungent. Hit solidly, Dimond was bumped against the far wall, his rifle going off in another deafening smash of sound, the bullet slamming into the ceiling, fetching down a cascade of dust; then Troy's second thundering shot abruptly doubled the rifleman over, eyes staring from his head, his moustache an incongruous slim pencil-line curving above his wide-open mouth. Dimond and his rifle went clumping to the floor, the room now swimming in gunsmoke.

French, coming fast now but still thirty feet short of the porch, caught a flick of movement to his left and in that instant saw the tall figure of

Purnell, pistol in hand. French, reacting with commendable speed, chopped his gunhand across and down, firing even as Purnell shot smokily at him, then Purnell was gone behind the corner of the house, for lead had breathed across his eyes out of the springing light of French's firing.

In the noise, the smoky confusion, Troy was struggling up from his chair, determined that if French came in he would confront him standing; but when he did manage to get to his feet and turn to the window that overlooked the yard, it was to see Purnell coming into view, no-one else anywhere in sight.

Purnell saw him and came up onto the porch and inside, casting a look at Dimond's body as he did. Troy said he was not hit, whereupon Purnell returned to the yard to try to discover where French had got to. To Troy, who had come shuffling out onto the porch, he called:

"Hit the bastard. There's blood on the grass here."

Striding quickly to them, Purnell looked inside a couple of the nearest outbuildings, knowing that French could not have got far, but finding nothing, then went down the other side of the house towards the front.

He was in time to see French, clearly struggling in his progress but some distance from Purnell now, almost out onto the Gabriel trail. French glanced back and upon seeing Purnell managed to increase his painful stride to vanish behind a clump of brush, obviously intent now on reaching one of the horses.

Purnell went jogging towards the place where he had last seen French, wary though, for he had no desire to discover, too late, that the man had stopped in his tracks, hurt but cunning, waiting for Purnell to come blundering onto the gun.

That cautious slowing of pace, cost Purnell the chance of nailing French, for by the time Purnell himself got out onto the trail, French, some way beyond the body of Pepperill, had whistled his own horse in and was in the act of mounting, the other horses having retreated even further.

Purnell stood — none too steadily after his exertions — drawing down, and the pistol bucked as he smoked a racketing shot away, but he knew as soon as it had gone that he had missed his man. French, too, had now managed to get the horse half turned and was thus screened from Purnell and had one boot up in a stirrup, hopping on the other as the horse moved, struggling to haul himself into the saddle. And then his leg did swing up over the cantle and he was in the saddle now and the horse was jumping away under him even as Purnell fired again amid acrid smoke, again without success, and was compelled to stand where he was, breathing strongly, pistol hanging by his side, having again paid the price for his urgent efforts with indifferent shooting.

The loosely-strung plans they had

made, however, had enjoyed more success than they could have dared hope for: if one of the hunters got isolated, Purnell would take him; if the chance arose they would draw them, one, two or all three if that was the only way, towards two guns when only one would have been expected.

The horseman, though sitting his saddle somewhat loosely, was heading towards Gabriel, no doubt intending to pass on through that place, but how badly wounded Purnell did not know. —Disconsolately Purnell began going in the direction of the two stray horses but they would have none of it, moving further away, so Purnell gave up and set out for Gabriel on foot. French, he must accept, was well away and what Purnell himself most wanted to do now was get to his own house to show that he was unharmed after all this shooting, and to reassure Imogen Troy about her father.

Vern Likens, having listened to that same gunfire, had been unable to settle.

The streets were as barren of people as they had been for most of this nerve-stretched morning, for the druggist's warnings had been taken seriously, as had the opinions of those who had actually set eyes on the sinister riders.

So Likens was standing in the doorway of his drugstore when he noticed the single horseman coming, and he could see also that this man, if not swaying in the saddle, did not look at all at ease, an odd, hunched aspect to his shoulders; and whoever he was he was riding with a pistol in one hand. Then with a lurch of apprehension Likens realized that he was staring at Jack French.

Likens did not remember picking up the 12-gauge, but as French drew nearer it was sure in his hands.

The next moment the window of the drugstore smashed into flying shards as a flick of flame stabbed from French's pistol and smoke went whipping away. Then Likens, in an angry reflex, had the long gun to his shoulder, tracking ahead of his Michigan game, and let fly a jolting, thudding report that tore its hurricane of lead-shot across the rider and whupped him sideways, blood flying as he went down, rolling in the thick mud of Main, the riderless horse galloping on strongly, reins flying.

Open-mouthed, Likens stood holding his shotgun tightly as, covered in mud, part of his face and his left shoulder shredded by the blast, but showing immense, malevolent strength, Jack French, sliding, trying to gain purchase for his boots, was coming slowly to his knees, the slime-covered pistol still gripped in one hand. Slowly the ugly black eye of the .44 came up to waver across Likens.

Long afterwards, the Gabriel druggist would anguish over the fear, the deep instinct for self-preservation, which caused him to level the shotgun again, to vent the second barrel at the man kneeling in the street.

Likens was still standing in that same place, holding the empty gun, when

Purnell came walking onto Main. He saw Likens there, then walked on to view what was left of the man the druggist had shotgunned.

Presently Purnell turned his back on the steaming, riven, bloodied body, the carcase of the man who had come here seeking Charlie Troy, and made his way across to Likens who, for the remainder of his life, would be spoken of and pointed out in streets as the man who had killed Jack French.

12

IN the night, Crimond had come and gone, hesitantly, not far short of penitently, with the object of sounding out Purnell, but had been sent on his way from the doorstep. No. No meetings before or after dark. No deals. *"If you're going in fear for your streets, strap a Colt on Henry."*

And carried lanterns, swinging their arcs of misted light, were to be seen around Edlin's. Gossip soon suggested that a notion had been floated to display the bodies of the notorious men, French and Dimond and Pepperill, in the dead-fly window of an empty store right on Main but when some of the townswomen happened to get wind of it, then if there was any substance to it, this plan was soon abandoned.

Lanterns were swinging, too, near the Purnell house, and again at a place called Croy's where for many months past several wagons, flotsam from a failed freighting concern, had stood among weeds awaiting offers; and had those with sufficient interest cared to look towards Cavan's, they would have seen lights bobbing around there as well.

By late evening, however, all these activities had ceased and an uneasy silence had again settled over Gabriel.

About mid-morning, under a still-overcast, smoky sky, a wagon hauled by a four-horse team came slowly off the trail and into Gabriel. Imogen Troy in her hooded blue cloak was driving it, and on the seat beside her was the wasted, waxen-skinned man, Charlie Troy, a grey blanket wrapped around his narrow shoulders and hooded over his head. The tensions and the danger-induced activities had all worked their various evils upon Troy and had left him much reduced physically, and at the present, noddingly somnolent, for earlier in the day he had been given medication by Vern Likens.

When the wagon came to the corner of a particular side-street Imogen looked across and waved, smiling, and almost at once, as though it had been waiting there, a second wagon came out from that street and drew in behind the Troy rig; but after they had gone only a short distance along Main, both were brought to a halt.

From the second wagon Purnell climbed down and walked on through mud and climbed up to sit beside Charlie Troy and unwound the reins from the brake-lever; for Imogen had quit the lead wagon and, long hair swinging, had gone back to the Purnell rig, Rob Purnell reaching down to help her up beside him and Mary.

Not a lot of people were abroad on Main, though now, at the appearance of wagons, a few indistinct faces had begun to show at windows. Likens, though, came out on the boardwalk and raised one of his pale hands to them; very pensive today, Likens.

"So you're going through with it, Brad."

"Yeah," Purnell said. "Got to make sure some friends get up there to Kansas."

Likens nodded soberly, gave another small motion of the hand and went back inside. Purnell felt immense compassion for the man, having to go on living in this place after all that had happened.

They would have moved on then, but Mary called, "Brad . . . Wait!"

Suddenly a number of women had come into view, some carrying covered baskets, others parcels wrapped in brown paper and tied with twine. Confidently, careless of the mud, these women came down off the boardwalks and presently groups formed near both wagons, more than twenty women in all, handing up gifts of preserves and other food and some parcels of clothing, mainly for Imogen. If the men of Gabriel, councillors and others, were aware of what was happening — and few could have been unaware — then not one of them ventured even as far as his damp doorway. Perhaps, Purnell thought sourly, it was sufficient that the risk of further infections arising from this scarecrow in the blanket was now being borne safely away. But it was more than enough that the women had come, for it marked for them too another line from which, as their very attitude was proclaiming, there was to be no retreat; and perhaps if, in the future, they ever thought of Charlie Troy, that would be how they would remember him.

Presently the wagons did move on, creaking, harness clinking, heading on out of Gabriel. At the very last corner, turning slowly around and around an awning-post, was a lone boy in a grey shirt and knickerbockers, Dave Schiller. He ceased his indolent rotations, watching them going by out of his crooked eyes.

Looking down at him, Rob raised a hand, then Imogen did too, and after a small hesitation Dave Schiller gave a kind of half wave and almost a grin, then went slouching away along the boardwalk, hands in pockets.

Rob Purnell and Imogen Troy exchanged calm looks, full of satisfaction and understanding, for suddenly it had occurred to both of them at precisely the same moment that it was important that they should leave not even one enemy behind them.

THE END

FIGHTING RAMROD
Charles N. Heckelmann

Most men would have cut their losses, but Frazer counted the bullets in his guns and said he'd soak the range in blood before he'd give up another inch of what was his.

LONE GUN
Eric Allen

Smoke Blackbird had been away too long. The Lequires had seized the Blackbird farm, forcing the Indians and settlers off, and no one seemed willing to fight! He had to fight alone.

THE THIRD RIDER
Barry Cord

Mel Rawlins wasn't going to let anything stand in his way. His father was murdered, his two brothers gone. Now Mel rode for vengeance.

ARIZONA DRIFTERS
W. C. Tuttle

When drifting Dutton and Lonnie Steelman decide to become partners they find that they have a common enemy in the formidable Thurston brothers.

TOMBSTONE
Matt Braun

Wells Fargo paid Luke Starbuck to outgun the silver-thieving stagecoach gang at Tombstone. Before long Luke can see the only thing bearing fruit in this eldorado will be the gallows tree.

HIGH BORDER RIDERS
Lee Floren

Buckshot McKee and Tortilla Joe cut the trail of a border tough who was running Mexican beef into Texas. They stopped the smuggler in his tracks.

BRETT RANDALL, GAMBLER
E. B. Mann

Larry Day had the choice of running away from the law or of assuming a dead man's place. No matter what he decided he was bound to end up dead.

THE GUNSHARP
William R. Cox

The Eggerleys weren't very smart. They trained their sights on Will Carney and Arizona's biggest blood bath began.

THE DEPUTY OF SAN RIANO
Lawrence A. Keating and
Al. P. Nelson

When a man fell dead from his horse, Ed Grant was spotted riding away from the scene. The deputy sheriff rode out after him and came up against everything from gunfire to dynamite.

FARGO: MASSACRE RIVER
John Benteen

The ambushers up ahead had now blocked the road. Fargo's convoy was a jumble, a perfect target for the insurgents' weapons!

SUNDANCE: DEATH IN THE LAVA
John Benteen

The Modoc's captured the wagon train and its cargo of gold. But now the halfbreed they called Sundance was going after it . . .

HARSH RECKONING
Phil Ketchum

Five years of keeping himself alive in a brutal prison had made Brand tough and careless about who he gunned down . . .

FARGO: PANAMA GOLD
John Benteen

With foreign money behind him, Buckner was going to destroy the Panama Canal before it could be completed. Fargo's job was to stop Buckner.

FARGO:
THE SHARPSHOOTERS
John Benteen

The Canfield clan, thirty strong were raising hell in Texas. Fargo was tough enough to hold his own against the whole clan.

PISTOL LAW
Paul Evan Lehman

Lance Jones came back to Mustang for just one thing — revenge! Revenge on the people who had him thrown in jail.

HELL RIDERS
Steve Mensing

Wade Walker's kid brother, Duane, was locked up in the Silver City jail facing a rope at dawn. Wade was a ruthless outlaw, but he was smart, and he had vowed to have his brother out of jail before morning!

DESERT OF THE DAMNED
Nelson Nye

The law was after him for the murder of a marshal — a murder he didn't commit. Breen was after him for revenge — and Breen wouldn't stop at anything . . . blackmail, a frameup . . . or murder.

DAY OF THE COMANCHEROS
Steven C. Lawrence

Their very name struck terror into men's hearts — the Comancheros, a savage army of cutthroats who swept across Texas, leaving behind a bloodstained trail of robbery and murder.

SUNDANCE: SILENT ENEMY
John Benteen

A lone crazed Cheyenne was on a personal war path. They needed to pit one man against one crazed Indian. That man was Sundance.

LASSITER
Jack Slade

Lassiter wasn't the kind of man to listen to reason. Cross him once and he'll hold a grudge for years to come — if he let you live that long.

LAST STAGE TO GOMORRAH
Barry Cord

Jeff Carter, tough ex-riverboat gambler, now had himself a horse ranch that kept him free from gunfights and card games. Until Sturvesant of Wells Fargo showed up.

McALLISTER ON THE COMANCHE CROSSING
Matt Chisholm

The Comanche, McAllister owes them a life — and the trail is soaked with the blood of the men who had tried to outrun them before.

QUICK-TRIGGER COUNTRY
Clem Colt

Turkey Red hooked up with Curly Bill Graham's outlaw crew. But wholesale murder was out of Turk's line, so when range war flared he bucked the whole border gang alone . . .

CAMPAIGNING
Jim Miller

Ambushed on the Santa Fe trail, Sean Callahan is saved by two Indian strangers. But there'll be more lead and arrows flying before the band join Kit Carson against the Comanches.

GUNSLINGER'S RANGE
Jackson Cole

Three escaped convicts are out for revenge. They won't rest until they put a bullet through the head of the dirty snake who locked them behind bars.

RUSTLER'S TRAIL
Lee Floren

Jim Carlin knew he would have to stand up and fight because he had staked his claim right in the middle of Big Ike Outland's best grass.

THE TRUTH ABOUT SNAKE RIDGE
Marshall Grover

The troubleshooters came to San Cristobal to help the needy. For Larry and Stretch the turmoil began with a brawl and then an ambush.

WOLF DOG RANGE
Lee Floren

Will Ardery would stop at nothing, unless something stopped him first — like a bullet from Pete Manly's gun.

DEVIL'S DINERO
Marshall Grover

Plagued by remorse, a rich old reprobate hired the Texas Trouble-shooters to deliver a fortune in greenbacks to each of his victims.

GUNS OF FURY
Ernest Haycox

Dane Starr, alias Dan Smith, wanted to close the door on his past and hang up his guns, but people wouldn't let him.